JACK'S MAGIC BEANS

BRIAN KEENE

deadite
press

deadite press

DEADITE PRESS
205 NE BRYANT
PORTLAND, OR 97211
www.DEADITEPRESS.com

AN ERASERHEAD PRESS COMPANY
www.ERASERHEADPRESS.com

ISBN: 1-936383-45-4

Acknowledgements

For this new edition of *Jack's Magic Beans*, my thanks to everyone at Deadite Press; Alan Clark; Monica Kuebler; Nate Lambert; Dennis Duncan; Sean and Francesca Lewis; Adam Brelsford; Tod Clark, Kelli Owen, Mark Sylva, and John Urbancik (who proofread the original version); Geoff Cooper (for Without You); J.F. Gonzalez (for The King in Yellow); Mary SanGiovanni; and my sons.

For Jim and Bonnie Moore . . .

CONTENTS

JACK'S
MAGIC
BEANS

ONE

The lettuce started talking to Ben Mahoney halfway through his shift at Save-A-Lot.

He'd shown up for work ten minutes late. Mr. Brubaker was waiting for him at the time clock.

"You're late, Mahoney."

Ben sighed. "Sorry, Mr. Brubaker. I had to stay late after school. I was talking to my teacher. Been having trouble with calculus."

This was bullshit. In fact, Ben had hung around to ask Stacy Gerlach if she'd go to Eleanor Murphy's party with him on Friday night. Eleanor's parents were in New York for the weekend on one of these bus trips where you got to go shopping and see a Broadway show. The party was supposed to be off the hook—two kegs and a DJ playing trance-hop all night long. Sadly, Stacy already had a date. Pissed off at this news, Ben had blown through two red lights on his way to work. He'd also blown his sub-woofer because the bass was cranked too high. Ben's bad day got worse, and his anger was still simmering when he rushed in.

He did not tell Mr. Brubaker any of this. Instead, he apologized and swore that it wouldn't happen again.

Scowling, hands on hips, Brubaker stomped away to holler at somebody else. Ben swiped his timecard, walked into the break room, pulled his smock out of his locker, and fished around in his pockets for loose change. He put four quarters into the soda machine, waited for the can to clunk down, popped the tab, took a sip, and then started his shift—all while trying to ignore the dull headache building behind his eyes.

Ben worked part-time in Save-A-Lot's produce department. He came in during the evenings and spent four hours rotating the fruit and vegetables—a process that involved pulling all of the produce out of the bins, placing fresh produce on the bottom, and then putting the older produce back on top. That way, customers would pick the older stuff first and it wouldn't go bad. The only problem with this method was that most of the people who shopped at Save-A-Lot knew about rotation and they invariably dug through the fruits and vegetables to the bottom of the bin, thus finding the fresher selections and fucking up all of his hard work.

Old people were especially bad about doing this, and that was one of the reasons Ben hated them. He also hated the way they walked and the way they smelled. He hated it when an old person was in front of him on the road. They didn't know how to drive. He hated it when they walked in front of him, blocking the aisle. He hated how they always bothered him with stupid questions when he was busy stocking shelves. He worked in the produce department. He knew where the apples were. Why, then, would they ask him where the spaghetti was located? You want to find the pasta? Try reading the fucking signs.

Ben was sixteen. He was physically and mentally fit—a teenaged Adonis. He would never get old. Never lose his hair or his hearing or control of his bladder. His joints and teeth would never ache. He would never have to worry about running out of breath from the simplest of tasks. His eyesight would never go bad. Neither would his internal organs. He would never have to worry about not being able to have an orgasm—let alone getting a hard-on. He was young and in his prime. These were the best years of his life and those years did not involve getting old. Old people filled him with loathing.

So when he saw the old woman squeezing the peaches, and the lettuce told him to kill her, Ben agreed. It seemed like a reasonable idea.

His headache got worse.

"Kill that old bitch," the heads of lettuce said in unison. They'd each grown a little mouth, the size of his thumbnail. Their voices were high-pitched, like a cartoon character. "Knock her over and kick her goddamned face in. Bet she's wearing dentures. No fucking way those teeth are real."

Ben dropped the spray bottle that he'd been using to mist the cucumbers. He stared at the lettuce. After a moment, he smiled, forgetting all about the pain behind his eyes. The lettuce smiled back at him.

12

"Go on, Ben," the lettuce urged. "Make her bleed."

"How do you know my name?"

"We are the lettuce. We know everything. It has always been thus and always will be. The lettuce is wise. Now kill that old bag."

It was hard to argue with lettuce. Like they'd said—they were wise. Shrugging, Ben dropped his apron on the floor, rushed across the store and knocked the old woman to the floor. Her head cracked against the linoleum. It sounded very loud. The sound made Ben smile. He kicked her in the side of her face. The old woman's dentures skittered beneath the banana display. The lettuce had been right. They weren't her real teeth.

The old woman pawed at his pants leg. Her eyes implored him.

Ben spit in her face. "You squeezed. The fucking. *Peaches.*"

Somebody screamed.

Ben giggled.

The old woman groaned.

Then Ben stomped her face again, harder this time. Her nose splintered beneath his heel. Ben realized that he had an erection. Rubbing himself through his jeans, he raised his foot and stomped a third time. And a fourth. Then he stood on top of her face with both feet and ground his soles back and forth, pushing down with all his weight. Something gave way beneath his feet. His shoes grew wet.

The old woman was the first to die. Ben died seconds later when Roger from the floral department skewered him through the chest with a broken mop handle. Roger laughed as he thrust the spear again. He stopped laughing and became the third to die when a customer ripped his tongue out with her bare hands.

Then everybody started dying at once.

Tom Brubaker had a headache and shouting made him feel better. After he was done hollering at Ben Mahoney, he shouted at the cashiers and the butchers and the baggers and a delivery guy and the little old Asian woman who ran the grocery store's Chinese kiosk. Then he yelled at Jeremy

Geist, the short, pudgy kid who was re-arranging the book and magazine display.

"Damn it, Geist. How many times do I have to tell you? Every book should be faced out. People are more likely to buy the fucking things if they can see the goddamned covers."

Mr. Brubaker arranged the books on the shelf so that the front covers were facing outward. "See? How hard is this?"

"I'm sorry, Mr. Brubaker."

Geist's bottom lip trembled. Brubaker focused on it, overcome with disgust. His headache intensified. His temples throbbed. Somebody screamed on the other side of the store. Brubaker ignored it. He said nothing. He didn't speak. Didn't holler. Didn't move.

Jeremy Geist thought that was worse—the not hollering part. He'd never seen Mr. Brubaker be quiet before. It made him nervous. He wondered who was screaming and why. Then more people started shrieking. There was some kind of commotion in the produce department. Things were getting weird. Shouldn't Mr. Brubaker be concerned about what was happening, rather than the book display? Jeremy, remembering some advice his counselor had given him on dealing with conflict, decided to reason with his boss.

"I knew I was supposed to face them out, sir. It's just that there's not enough room. There are too many books and not enough space in the display."

While Jeremy had been talking, Brubaker had been staring at the books. He'd barely heard a word the young employee said. His protests and explanations were like the buzzing of insects. Now that Jeremy was done, Mr. Brubaker grinned.

The screams grew louder.

Brubaker's headache vanished. He glanced back to the shelves. Each of the paperbacks had the same title: *KILL 'EM ALL*.

It was very sound advice. After all, these were bestsellers written by important authors who knew what they were talking about. Oprah said these books had meaning and value. Oprah said these books would enrich your life. You couldn't argue with Oprah. That was crazy.

14

So he didn't. Instead, Brubaker wrapped his hands around Jeremy Geist's throat and squeezed. Geist's lip began trembling again, so Brubaker squeezed harder to make it stop. It did. The lip stopped trembling, and then Jeremy stopped breathing. A few feet away from them, a customer overturned the magazine rack onto a little girl. Then the customer hopped onto the rack and jumped up and down. The child, still pinned beneath the wreckage, blood leaking from her mouth, screamed in anguish and terror for her mother. Her mother didn't answer, because her mother was too busy shouting obscenities and clawing the face of another customer. She raked her fingernails deep, gouging furrows in the flesh.

Brubaker remained oblivious. He focused on Jeremy and kept squeezing, even after Geist was dead.

He didn't stop squeezing until another customer squirted him with lighter fluid and set him on fire.

Mr. Brubaker laughed as he burned. The more intense the flames became, the louder his laughter grew.

Angela Waller was third in line at the pharmacy counter when the screaming started. She flinched, almost dropping her purse. The redneck guy in front of her was startled enough by the commotion to stop arguing with the pharmacist. Angie paused, waiting for gunshots—expecting maybe a robbery or some disgruntled nutcase on a rampage. When the gunshots didn't come, she held her breath. The screams got louder.

Behind her, somebody said, "I wish they'd shut up. My head hurts."

It had been a weird afternoon—getting weirder with each second. Angie had seen more road rage and rudeness on her way here than she normally saw in a month. There was something in the air, something heavy and malignant, ready to burst like storm clouds bloated with rain. If there was trouble in the store, then Angie wanted no part of it. She just wanted to get her prescription filled and go home, where she'd take off her work clothes, put on some pajama pants, curl up on the bed, and paint her toenails.

In three days, Angie and her girlfriends were taking a

cruise to Antigua in celebration of her twenty-ninth birthday. Girls only—no boyfriends or husbands. She needed her Prozac before she left. That was the only reason she remained in line when the screams began. The pills were a necessity, just like tampons, her diaphragm, her passport, and cell phone. Prozac: don't leave home without it. She'd been diagnosed with chronic depression when she was fifteen, and had been on the drug most of her adult life. Sure, the recommended length of usage was only six to twelve months, but like her doctor said, if it helped, it helped. And help it did. She could function on Prozac. Taking it was as natural as breathing.

The screams increased, multiplying throughout the store.

And then Angie forgot all about Antigua and her prescription because the pharmacist lunged over the counter and stabbed his pen into the neck of the man in front of her. The redneck reared back, grasping at the pen. A little bit of blood bubbled out around it, but not as much as Angie would have expected. The redneck made a startled, squawking sort of sound. Humming the theme from *The Young and the Restless*, the pharmacist grappled with the injured man. Angie backed away from them, too frightened to scream, and this time she did drop her purse. Doing so saved her life. She knelt to pick it up and thus avoided a sweeping blow from the woman behind her, who had decided to crack Angie in the back of the head with a bottle of green mouthwash.

"You slept with my Herbert," the woman shouted. "Little whore!"

Angie tried to skitter backwards, but there was nowhere to go. All around her, fights broke out. Customers and Save-A-Lot employees clawed, punched, and shrieked at each other. A naked fat man crawled around on all fours, growling like a dog. A severed penis dangled from his clenched teeth. A woman tried swinging from the skylights but crashed to the floor. A crowd of people leapt on her, tearing her to shreds with their bare hands. Another woman with a nail file sticking out of her breast ran past, screaming about a gnome in her tiramisu. Blood flowed—pooling on the floor, splashing across displays, pouring from wounds, and staining the hands, mouths, feet, and makeshift weapons of the attackers.

"You fucked Herbert! You fucked him hard!"

Angie's attacker kicked her in the side. Slipping in a puddle of liquid soap and someone else's blood, Angie curled into a ball and tried to protect herself. The woman yelled again, once more accusing Angie of sleeping with Herbert, but Angie was pretty sure she'd never slept with a Herbert, married or otherwise. She tried to tell her attacker that, but all that came out was a whimper.

"Did he lick you?" the woman shrieked. "He never did that for me. The son of a bitch. He never once licked me. He said he didn't like it. But I know the truth. He couldn't find the clit."

"Please," Angie rasped. "I don't—"

The woman aimed another kick, and Angie focused on staying alive.

Marcel Dupree had just turned off his car and was double-checking the headlights, radio, and everything else when somebody rear-ended him. The impact bounced him off the steering column, knocking the wind from his lungs. Shocked, Marcel flung the door open and stumbled outside, forgetting all about the headlights. He was too flustered to speak. He could only watch in stunned silence as a black Cadillac Escalade reversed, then raced forward and rammed his car again. The SUV's driver was hidden behind tinted windows.

"Hey," Marcel tried to shout. It came out more like a whisper. The driver gave no indication that they'd heard him. The Cadillac's engine roared and smoke belched from the tailpipe.

The impact of the collision slammed his car door shut. Marcel wondered if the door was locked. As the Cadillac backed up, he checked the door and then checked it again. He was about to check a third time, when he became dimly aware that other people were hollering, as well. He heard the distinct impact of another car crash. Sirens wailed—police, fire, and ambulance. Marcel glanced around, trying to determine what was happening. The Cadillac ran into his car again, crumpling the rear bumper.

"Hey," Marcel shouted, finally finding his voice. "What are you doing?"

Forgetting about the door lock, he ran towards the Escalade, waving his fists and yelling. The tinted window slid down, revealing the driver. Marcel had never seen him before.

"What the hell is your problem, man?"

"You took my parking space!" Spittle flew from the enraged driver's mouth. His face was red. "How do you like it? Huh, motherfucker? How do you fucking like it, nigger?"

The racial slur shocked Marcel. He'd been called it before, when he was younger, but the word still had impact. Before he could respond, the Cadillac's driver turned the wheel and sped towards him. Marcel leapt out of the way and rolled across the hot pavement. Then he jumped to his feet and shouted for help. All around him, people ran through the parking lot. Most of them were engaged in similar battles, fighting in groups or one-on-one, using vehicles, shopping carts, tire irons, and anything else as weapons. He gaped in horror as a pick-up truck ran over a fleeing mother pushing a baby stroller, then reversed and ran over them again. The vehicle bounced up and down as the tires rolled over the corpses. A young man with a pistol shot the truck's driver and then turned the gun on other bystanders. Some charged him, some ran away, and others totally ignored the assault, involved as they were in other fights. A cop shot the young man with the gun, blowing his lungs through his back. The officer then fired at an old woman beating a teenager over the head with her walker.

"Police!" Marcel tried to get the cop's attention. "Over here. Help!"

The cop wheeled around, attracted by his cries. Marcel's relief vanished as the cop aimed the pistol at him.

"No!" Marcel held his hands up in surrender. "What are you—"

A neon-green Volkswagen slammed into the cop. The policeman flipped up over the hood, smashing against the windshield. His shoes remained on the pavement—his feet still inside them. The blacktop turned red. Inside the car, four teenage girls laughed. Then they turned on each other, clawing and gouging. The Volkswagen crashed into a parked car.

Marcel fought the urge to puke. There were angry cries behind him. He ran for the Save-A-Lot, aware that people were suddenly chasing him, shouting things—threats, curses, promises. He focused on counting his steps.

One . . . two . . . three . . .

His heart pounded. His mouth went dry. His lungs burned with the exertion. More feet echoed behind him as others joined in the chase.

Thirteen . . . fourteen . . . oh God . . . fifteen . . .

He burst through the doors of Save-A-Lot and skidded to a halt. Normally, Marcel would have spent the next five minutes trying to select the right shopping cart. But today, his disorder was all but forgotten. He felt the urge to call his doctor and tell him he'd found a cure. After all the frustration and the constant experimenting with different medicines, he'd found a way to beat it.

He didn't need meds. He just needed chaos. Chaos and disorder.

Marcel stood staring at the scene inside the store.

If the parking lot had been a battleground, this was the frontline.

And then the war *really* started.

Sammi Barberra had just closed out her register, and was getting ready to turn in her cash drawer and clock out, when everybody in the store went insane. It started with one scream, then six, then a dozen. Fights broke out across the store. There was a lot of savagery, and a lot of blood. An explosion in the parking lot rocked the building on its foundation, and for one moment, Sammi feared the ceiling might collapse. The overhead lights flickered, swaying violently back and forth, but stayed on. One of the big panel windows at the front of the store shattered, spraying shards of glass all over the floor—and all over the customers who had been fighting in front of it. Sammi ducked down behind the register, huddling into a ball and trying to remain out of sight while all around her, people slaughtered each other. She put her hands over her ears, attempting to block the screams, the cries, the impact of flesh on flesh—and the wet, tearing sounds. Another explosion rumbled from farther away. Somebody shrieked for God to come save them.

Sammi stayed where she was, hidden from view. The only problem was, she couldn't see what was happening now. Sammi peeked around the corner of the counter and immediately wished she hadn't.

Mr. Brubaker's burned head rolled slowly across the floor. Sammi resisted the urge to scream. The manager's eyes and mouth were still open. A customer was bowling with it, using plastic milk jugs as pins and Mr. Brubaker's head as the ball. Even though his flesh was burned, Sammi still recognized her supervisor's severed head. It came to rest at the foot of the candy rack in her aisle. His head was upside down and she could see into the ragged stump, straight down his windpipe. Mr. Brubaker's eyes stared at her. He looked angry, even in death. Sammi ducked back beneath the register and bit her lip to keep from crying out.

"Damn," she heard the bowler mutter. "I need more balls."

There was a brief moment of silence. The crazy person had apparently moved on.

She needed to pee. She squeezed her thighs together and wept silent tears. She bit her lip harder.

Footsteps drew towards her.

"Oh God . . ."

Sammi jumped to her feet, preparing to flee. Before she could get out from behind the register, somebody grabbed her wrist and yanked her forward over the counter. It was Jerry Sadler, the retarded guy who collected shopping carts in the parking lot and sometimes bagged groceries for customers. Sammi didn't recognize him at first, because one of Jerry's ears was missing and there was a wide gash in his cheek, deep enough to reveal his teeth and gums. Pain shot up her arm.

"Jerry," she gasped. "Let go, you're hurting me. Are you okay?"

"You're so pretty. I always thought you were pretty."

His words were slurred as a result of his injury, but his eyes shone with clear intent.

"Jerry!" Sammi tried to pull away, but he tightened his grip.

"You're too skinny, though. It makes you look younger. Makes you look like a little girl."

"Stop it!"

"I like little girls. I like them a lot. I watch them all the time."

"Get off me, you freak."

In the next register aisle, a child in a brightly-colored Spongebob shirt sprayed a wounded, quivering woman in the face with a can of hornet spray. The chemical stench filled the air. The spray bubbled, foamy and white, mingling with the woman's blood. The pint-sized maniac giggled. The woman screamed, clawing at her eyes. Sammi began to cry. She turned her attention back to he co-worker.

"Jerry, you're hurting me. Stop it."

"You called me a freak," Jerry said. "I know what that is. I'm not stupid. Freak—that's like a retard. You called me a retard."

"I'm sorry, okay?" Sammi tried to reason with him. "We've got to get away, Jerry. We've got to get out of here. Something's wrong. Please let go."

A man stumbled by them. He was bent over, clutching his stomach. The handle of an umbrella jutted from his back. He didn't pay them any attention, muttering instead about wanting to go swimming in a vat of tapioca pudding.

"Look how skinny your wrist is," Jerry slurred. "I can snap your bones, just like a little bird."

He smiled. A thin line of pink drool dripped from his bottom lip and landed on the counter. Nearby, an injured employee crawled towards them on her hands and knees. Sammi couldn't tell who it was because the woman's face, hands, and name badge were covered in blood.

"Jerry," Sammi warned. "Let me go."

Still smiling, Jerry twisted her wrist. Another sharp jolt of pain shot up Sammi's arm. Screaming, she slapped at him, but Jerry dodged the blow. With her free hand, Sammi grabbed her cash drawer. Then she lashed out with it, striking him in his already wounded face. Teeth shattered. Jerry let go of her wrist and moaned, shaking with rage. Sammi hit him again. He struck out, backhanding the drawer. It flew from Sammi's grip and clattered across the floor.

"Gonna break all your little bones, skinny girl."

A broken tooth fell out of his mouth as he made the threat. Jerry didn't seem to notice. He made another grab for Sammi's wrist, but then the crawling employee reached them. This close, Sammi could see her features through the blood. She recognized her as Hazel Stern, one of the supervisors who usually worked the service desk. Sammi didn't know her very well. Rumor around the store was that Hazel and Mr. Brubaker were having an affair. Sammi also glimpsed the scissors clutched in the injured woman's hand. Without pausing, Hazel stabbed them into Jerry's leg, cooing softly as she did.

Shrieking, Jerry turned his wrath on the new opponent. As the two employees struggled, Sammi vaulted over the counter and fled down the aisle, dodging attackers and leaping over corpses. A jar of spaghetti sauce whizzed by her head, smashing into a row of pickles. A customer tried to push a breakfast cereal display over on her, but she dodged the falling boxes and kept running.

A little boy lay sprawled on his stomach in front of her. Blood trickled from one of his ears. As she passed by, he reached for her, his tone pleading.

"Please, help me."

Sammi paused, but before she could act, an adult grabbed the child's feet and dragged him away.

"Come on, kid. Let's get you on the butcher's block."

The boy wailed. His eyes remained on Sammi. Weeping, Sammi kept going, heading towards the rear of the store. There was nothing she could do.

Not for the first time today, she felt like throwing up. The only difference was that this time, she hadn't eaten.

And then there was Jack Bartlett, who spent his fifteen-minute break bundled up in a heavy coat, taking a nap inside the meat department's big walk-in freezer.

Jack missed the whole thing.

TWO

When Jack woke up, people were screaming.

Several of them, judging by the sound.

He opened his eyes and sat up straight, banging his head against the cold steel wall. Wincing, he blinked, trying to figure out what was happening. There were two women in the freezer with him. That accounted for the screaming. One of the women was about his age, startlingly skinny and wearing a Save-A-Lot uniform just like his. Her long, blonde hair was pulled into a ponytail with a neon-pink scrunchy. The other woman was older, maybe in her late twenties, dressed in jeans and a white, spaghetti-strap blouse. Her short, brunette hair was plastered to her scalp with sweat and blood. Jack didn't know her, but he definitely knew the skinny girl—Sammi Barberra, one of the cashiers. She was a freshman at the community college, just like him. His buddy, Phil, had gone out with her a few times back in high school. Rumor was that Sammi had bulimia. Looking at her, it was easy to believe. She was pretty, in a super-model-goes-to-Auschwitz sort of way. Definitely not his type.

Both women continued yelling and crying, and Jack realized that they were trying to hold the door shut. Somebody was pounding on the other side, hollering to be let in. The blows echoed through the freezer, loud enough to be heard over their cries. Neither Sammi nor the other woman seemed to have noticed Jack. Their backs were to him. Both of them gripped the door handle tightly and kept pulling it shut, bracing their feet apart. There was blood on their clothes. Their panic was palpable.

Jack sat up the rest of the way and said, "Hey."

Ignoring him, they kept their attention focused on the door.

"Pull," the woman shouted. "Pull!"

"I'm trying," Sammi sobbed. "Oh my God . . ."

Outside, whoever was pounding on the door hollered, "Let me in, god damn it! They're gonna kill me."

"Stay out there," the woman yelled. "Don't you come in here."

23

"Please, listen to me! I'm okay. I'm not like the others. You've got to let me in!"

"Just go away." Sammi grunted, pulling harder. "Leave us alone!"

Jack stood up. His heavy freezer coat rustled. "Hey," he tried again. "What's going on?" The women screamed in unison. Sammi let go of the door handle and turned around. The other woman held tight but looked over her shoulder. Smiling in confusion, Jack took a step towards them, hands held out in front of him, palms up, to show that he meant no harm.

Sammi's eyes grew wide. "Stay back. Just stay away from us. Don't come any closer!"

He stopped. "Sammi, it's me—Jack. Phil's friend? What the hell are you doing? What are you afraid of?"

Before she could answer, the door was wrenched out of the other woman's hands. A black man ran into the freezer. His clothes were also spattered with blood.

"Shut it," he yelled. "Shut the door, quick!"

"Are you one of them," the woman demanded. "Are you okay?"

"I'm fine," he said. "Do I look like I'm trying to claw your eyeballs out? I told you before, I'm, not like the others. Now shut the god damn door."

Jack heard more screams from outside the freezer. Lots of them. Wide-awake now, he took another cautious step forward while the woman slammed the freezer door shut again.

"What's going on?" Jack asked. "Is somebody hurt?"

"Who the hell are you?" The man whirled around, fists raised.

"Who the hell am I? I work here. My name's Jack. And unless I'm mistaken, customers aren't allowed in the freezer. So who the fuck are *you*?"

"Marcel. And you just stay right there, man. Don't make me hurt you. I'll mess you up."

Shaking his head, Jack turned to Sammi. "What's going on?"

"They . . . the people . . . Mr. Brubaker . . . Jerry tried to . . ."

24

She broke off, sobbing.

"Somebody help me with this door," the other woman said. "Is there a way to lock it?"

"It's a safety door," Jack told her. "Can't lock it from the inside, just so nobody accidentally gets trapped. You can lock it from the outside, but even then, somebody inside the freezer can still open it. But why do you need to lock it?"

"Duh. So they don't get in. Haven't you been listening?"

Jack took a deep breath. "Who? Who is *they*? Where did all this blood come from? Who's hurt?"

Sammi wiped her nose on her apron. "A lot of people. Hurt or dead."

"Look . . ." Jack ran his hands through his hair. "I don't understand this. What the hell is happening?"

"First the door," Marcel said. "Otherwise, we're not going to be around long enough to tell you."

A quick search of the freezer turned up several lengths of plastic strapping bands that had been used to fasten boxes to skids. There was also a large roll of shrink-wrap. While the women held the door closed, Jack and Marcel tied it shut with the plastic bands and makeshift shrink-wrap rope—running them from the doorknob to a nearby shelf, thus making it hard for anyone outside to pull open the door. As they finished, someone else pounded on the door. Unintelligible moans and shrieks accompanied the blows. Fingernails screeched across steel. The four survivors stared at the door, not daring to speak, barely breathing. After a few minutes, the sounds faded.

"Sounds like a zombie movie out there," Jack said.

"You don't know the half of it," Marcel replied.

"Jesus," the older woman panted. "I can't believe this."

"Quiet," Sammi whispered. "They might still be out there."

"You're right. Sorry."

Sammi shrugged. "It's okay. What's your name?"

"Angie. Angie Waller." She winced, gently rubbing her side.

"Are you okay?" Sammi asked.

Angie nodded. "I'll be fine. Some old lady kicked me in the ribs, but I don't think they're broken."

"I'm Sammi. This is Jack." She turned to the black man. "And what did you say your name was?"

"Marcel." He moved past them and checked the door, fingering the bands and shrink-wrap ropes, making sure they were tight and secure. "Marcel Dupree."

"It'll hold," Jack said to Marcel. "I was in the Scouts. I know how to tie a knot."

Marcel didn't answer. His attention remained focused on the door.

"So," Jack sighed. "Are you guys going to tell me what's going on or not?"

"How can you not know?" Angie asked.

"I was taking a nap. What did I sleep through?"

They told him.

THREE

They remained inside the freezer for the next hour, huddled together for warmth and whispering, careful not to attract attention. Occasionally, someone on the outside would try the door, but the makeshift bonds held. Eventually, the screams and cries subsided. Angie, Marcel, and Sammi all had cell phones with them, but when they tried to dial for help, none of them could get a signal since they were surrounded by steel walls.

Shivering, Sammi clasped her arms around her shoulders. "It's cold in here."

"It's a freezer," Jack said. "It's supposed to be cold."

Their breath hung in the air like wisps of fog when they spoke. The compressor hummed softly on the other side of the wall.

"Besides," he continued, "it could be worse."

"How?" Sammi asked. "What could possibly be any worse than this?"

"The lights could go out."

"Actually," Marcel said, "that's a good point. We know the power is still on. Otherwise the freezer wouldn't be running. So if the electricity is still on, then maybe this didn't happen everywhere. Maybe it was just confined to Save-A-Lot."

"I don't know," Angie said. "Even on the way here, people seemed angrier than normal. On the highway. I didn't realize it at first, but looking back now, I remember it. There was a lot of road rage. And we all heard fire sirens and police cars. They weren't all coming here. If they had been, we'd have seen them arrive."

Marcel snorted. "So everybody all over the world just went insane at the same fucking time? That's what you're saying?"

"Maybe not all over the world." Angie shrugged. "But at least here in town. Could be it's some sort of localized thing."

"Yeah," Jack said, "but what kind of thing? I mean, what

27

makes everyone go bat-shit crazy all at once and start killing each other?"

"Terrorists." Marcel got to his feet. "Al Qaeda, or maybe some homegrown group like those Sons of the Constitution motherfuckers. Maybe they dropped some gas on us."

"How?"

"They could have used a crop-duster or something. Like what happened in that little town in Pennsylvania a few years ago. That chemical got released from a hot air balloon and made the rain purple, and then everybody died? Supposedly they all went insane before they were killed. Remember that?"

"I do," Sammi whispered. "I had nightmares about it for weeks. Those poor people . . ."

"It couldn't be gas," Jack said, watching Marcel as he crossed the freezer and checked the door again. The man seemed to be counting his steps under his breath. "If it had been, you guys would have smelled it when it came through the store's ventilation system."

"Not necessarily," Angie said. "Gas can be odorless and invisible. But I agree that it wasn't gas. It was windy outside. If they'd used gas, some of it would have blown away. If that happened, then it wouldn't have been as effective in the parking lot, and the way Marcel talks, things were just as bad out there right before he came in. And besides, if there was gas, then each of us would have breathed it and gone nuts, too—and we're okay."

"Maybe we're immune," Jack suggested.

"You can't be immune to gas."

"The water, then." Sammi's teeth chattered as she spoke. She rubbed her arms briskly. "Somebody could have spiked the town's water supply."

"Maybe," Angie agreed, watching Marcel. "But I drank water from the tap today, and took a shower, too, and I didn't go crazy. How about you?"

"I don't drink city water," Sammi said. "I only use bottled spring water."

"But you showered, right? Brushed your teeth?"

Sammi nodded. "Yeah, after my morning run."

"Well, there you go."

Jack noticed Sammi's face turn red, as if she were embarrassed. He wondered why. Sammi looked away from them. Jack turned his attention back to Marcel. He was checking the straps again.

"What's up, Marcel?"

He shrugged. "Just making sure these will hold."

"Dude, they're okay. I told you, I'm the knot master. You keep messing with them, somebody on the other side is going to hear you."

"I know." But even as he said it, Marcel gave no indication of stopping. He tugged the bonds again. "Just want to be sure."

"Marcel . . ."

"I can't help it, kid. Leave me be."

"My name's Jack. Not kid."

Releasing the bands, Marcel turned around and walked back to them.

"I'm sorry," he said. "Guess I should have said something sooner. It's just a little embarrassing is all—especially telling strangers."

They stared at him, but it was Jack who finally spoke up, asking what they were all thinking.

"What is?"

Marcel sat down again. "I've got OCD—Obsessive Compulsive Disorder. That's why I was fucking with the straps. You guys know what OCD is?"

They nodded.

"Of course you do," he muttered. "Everybody does these days. People make jokes about it at work and on TV. Most people think that folks with OCD are crazy. But we're not—and it ain't funny. I hate being like this. Hate the fucking looks people give me."

"So your OCD has to do with doors?" Angie asked.

Marcel nodded. "Yeah, something like that. Doors and appliances, mostly. I need to make sure the doors are locked and everything is turned off. That's what I was doing when . . . well, when everything went to shit. I was sitting in my car, double-checking the headlights and stuff. The more stressed

I am, the worse it is, and right now, I'm pretty fucking stressed. I'm scared and worried about my family and I'm sick of sitting in here freezing my ass off. But at the same time, I know it's suicide to go back out there. So, my OCD kicked in and I was making sure the straps around the doors are secure. We know they are. Your knots will probably hold. But I've got to make sure anyway. I can't help it. And it ain't just doors, either. I have to count things—how many potato chips I eat out of the bag, how many steps I take, how many times the phone rings. And I can't stand odd numbers. Like, if I'm reading a book, I can't stop on an odd numbered page. If I walk somewhere, I have to end on an even numbered step. When I'm channel surfing, I skip past the odd-numbered channels. If I go out to eat and the check comes and it's an odd number, I've got to tip enough to make it even."

They stared at him, not speaking.

Marcel shrugged. "I guess you probably think I'm crazy."

"I don't," Jack said. "Shit, man—we've all got our problems, you know? I'm on Prozac. People make fun of that, too."

Marcel grinned. "Prozac? So am I. It's the only thing that works for me. I tried Paxil, Luvox, Xanax, and Zoloft, but all they did was make me comatose. So now I'm on Prozac. It works better."

"Not to be rude," Angie said, "but if you're checking the door even though you know it's secured, then are you sure the medicine is working? Maybe you need a different dosage."

"Yeah. Believe me, I'm sure it's working. Like I said, my symptoms get worse when I'm stressed. So pardon me if I seem a little freaked out right now."

Outside the door, somebody screamed—a long, unwavering howl that seemed to rise in pitch and intensity. Then it stopped.

"Fuck," Jack whispered. "That sounded like some kind of animal. Are you guys sure it was other people that did these things?"

"You didn't see them." Angie burst into tears. "I'm not surprised they sound like animals."

She lowered her head and sobbed. Her shoulders shook, but she made no sound.

"Hey." Marcel reached out a tentative hand and squeezed her shoulder. "If you're worried you offended me with that medicine remark, don't be."

"No," she sobbed. "It's not that. I'm just scared. And depressed. Story of my life. I've got chronic depression. You guys aren't the only two people on Prozac. That's what I was here for, too."

Marcel nodded. "Me, too. I ran out of meds yesterday, in fact. Haven't taken any since yesterday morning. Come to think of it, that might be why my OCD symptoms are a little worse today. I was on my way in here to pick up my prescription."

Angie wiped her eyes on her sleeve.

"That's kind of weird," Marcel continued. "Right? That all three of us would be taking Prozac?"

"Not really," Jack said. "There are lots of people on Prozac these days, dude. The doctors prescribe it like candy."

"Yeah, but to have three people out of four on it? That just seems odd to me."

"Four," Sammi mumbled.

"What's that?"

"Four people on Prozac. I take it, too."

"You're depressed?" Jack asked.

Sammi shook her head.

Marcel let go of Angie's shoulder. "OCD?"

"No." Sammi sighed, pausing before she spoke again. "Bulimia."

"I knew it," Jack said, then stopped, realizing he'd blurted it out. His mouth hung open. His cheeks reddened with shame.

"Knew what?" Sammi snapped.

"Just . . . well, some of the guys back in high school said that you were anorexic. That was why you were so skinny. Phil, too. I'm sorry. I shouldn't have said anything."

"You should be sorry. And I'm not anorexic. I'm bulimic. There's a difference between the two, you know. And I'm getting help. That's why I'm on Prozac."

"So . . . you throw up after you eat?" Now that the rumor had been confirmed, Jack was honestly curious.

"No. Not that it's any of your fucking business, but I'm an exercise bulimic. I used to binge—I mean, eat— and then I'd exercise my ass off. At first, I thought it was a healthy, competitive way to lose weight. I had lots of energy—like I'd just chugged a can of Red Bull. It felt good, you know? When the endorphin rush kicked in, I wasn't depressed anymore. Didn't feel bad about myself. And most importantly, I looked toned. But I wasn't toned. I was just building muscle while I dehydrated myself to burn off the fat. My skin clung more closely to my muscles. People tried talking to me about it, but I wouldn't listen. Finally, I got real sick. Passed out at a rave. My doctor prescribed Prozac to curb my desire to binge, since food is a form of comfort. I've been taking that and going to counseling for six weeks now."

"Six weeks," Jack said. "Must be nice. I've been on Prozac most of my life."

"That's dangerous," Marcel warned.

"I know. But the doctor said if it's working, then we should stick with it."

"Maybe you're better off," Marcel admitted. "There is a crazy side effect when you stop taking it. At least there was for me. I got horrible vertigo—like someone just pulled the floor out from under me. It lasted for a couple weeks, totally at random. At least you didn't have to go through that."

"I started taking it when I was ten," Jack said. "I didn't want to at first. Thought it meant I was crazy or something. My Mom coaxed me, though. She used to call the pills 'magic beans'. You know, like in *Jack and the Beanstalk?*"

The other nodded.

"She said my depression was like a big giant, and if I took my magic beans, then I'd have a way to defeat it. The doctor liked that. In fact, he liked it so much that I think he started using it on other kids, too. He told me to visualize the beanstalk as a line to recovery and wellness. My cure was waiting at the top of the beanstalk—a castle in the clouds. He was always spouting psychobabble bullshit like that. Weird old geezer. I don't go to him anymore, but my new doctor has me on Prozac, too."

Marcel chuckled, then broke into laughter. It echoed in the freezer, bouncing off the walls. The others stared at him in shock, dismayed by his bizarre reaction.

"Dude," Jack whispered. "Stop it or they'll hear you."

Still laughing, Marcel put his hands over his mouth and squeezed his eyes shut.

"Asshole," Sammi pouted. "You're just as fucked up as we are. What gives you the right to laugh at Jack?"

Marcel paused, catching his breath. "I'm not laughing at him. Seriously."

"Well, then what's so funny?"

"Us." He gestured at them. "We're all on Prozac. We're stigmatized by society because of it. Think about it. Everybody in town goes fucking insane, and the only four people left alive and apparently immune are people who all suffer from some form of mental illness. Everybody else used to think we were crazy. Suddenly, we ain't so fucking crazy anymore. We're the sane ones."

Marcel giggled again. Angie smiled. After a moment, Sammi did, too. Both women began to laugh. Jack didn't say anything. His expression was serious. After a moment, the others noticed.

"What's wrong?" Angie asked. "Did you hear something?"

"No," he whispered, "but I think I figured out why we're still alive—why we're immune to whatever made everyone else go nuts."

"Why?"

He grinned. "The magic beans."

All three of them stared at him.

"Prozac," he explained. "Remember? I said my Mom used to call them magic beans?"

"Yeah," Sammi said. "What about it."

"It's the one thing we all have in common. We all took Prozac today."

"I didn't," Marcel reminded him. "I'd run out."

"Yeah, but you still take it regularly. We all do. And I bet there were other people out there who were on it, too. Think about it. Was everybody crazy?"

"I saw a little boy," Sammi said, her voice trembling. "He asked me to help him, but before I could . . ." She trailed off, unable to finish.

"I saw people, too," Angie confirmed. "They seemed fine—scared, like me."

Marcel nodded. "Same here."

"I bet they were like us," Jack said. "Bet they were on Prozac."

"You don't know that," Angie said. "There are too many variables. Dosage. Type. Things like that."

Jack shrugged. "I'm on pills. What about the rest of you?"

"Pills," Angie said.

"Liquid." Sammi shivered. "But it can't be the Prozac. That doesn't make any sense."

"It makes about as much sense as everybody else suddenly turning into homicidal fucking maniacs. Didn't you ever have Mrs. Repasky's biology class?"

"No." Sammi shook her head. "I had Mr. Jackson. He's gross. He was always biting his fingernails and then spitting them all over the floor while he talked."

"Yeah, I never liked him."

"Me either."

"Mrs. Repasky," Jack said, "told us about how diseases change over time. With each generation, some new and terrible disease pops up. The Black Death, leprosy, cholera, cancer, Aids. That flu strain that killed all those people after World War One. All of these illnesses came out of nowhere, with no warning, and infected millions. So what if mental illnesses suddenly started doing the same thing? What if they mutated?"

Angie snorted. "You're saying that all those people were infected by some bizarre new psychosis?"

"Maybe," Jack said. "And we're immune to it because of the Prozac."

Sammi shook her head. "Is that even possible?"

"Shit." Jack shrugged. "How the hell do I know? I'm just a stock boy."

THREE

"I hope my family is okay." Sammi's nose had turned from red to white, and tiny ice crystals clung to her eyelashes. "I promised my little sister I'd help her with her homework tonight. She's in eighth grade."

Without warning, she started to cry again.

"Try not to think about it," Marcel said. "Ain't nothing we can do for them right now."

Angie frowned. "That's pretty cold, don't you think?"

"No," Marcel said. "It's not cold. Just practical. I got people at home, too. And I know they'd want me to stay alive."

"Cold . . ." Sammi sniffled. "It's so cold in here."

The others nodded in agreement. Jack stood up, stretched his stiff arms and legs, and crept to the door. He put his ear close to the frigid metal and listened.

"Hear anything?" Marcel asked.

"No. Nothing. It's quiet. Seriously, guys—it's been a while since we heard anything. Maybe they're all gone—or dead."

"Maybe," Marcel said, "or could be it's just a trap. Maybe they're waiting right outside the door."

"Well," Angie whispered, "we can't stay in here much longer. That's for sure. We'll get frostbite, not to mention there's no food or water—unless you count that frozen stuff. And pretty soon, I'm going to have to go to the bathroom."

Marcel pointed to the corner. "Go ahead. Knock yourself out. We won't look."

"No thanks. I can hold it a little while longer."

"I'm staying put," Marcel said. "You guys will too, if you're smart."

Jack returned to the group and hunkered down on his haunches. "Screw that. I'm not starving to death inside a grocery store freezer. I'd rather take my chances out there."

"Same here," Sammi said. "I want to see my family. I want my Mom."

"One step at a time," Jack told her. "First we have to get out of this freezer."

Marcel sighed. "Oh fuck me running. I'm not going to be able to talk you guys out of this, am I?"

"No," Jack said, "but we won't blame you if you want to stay behind. We'll send help, soon as we find some. I promise."

Angie pulled out her cell phone and flipped it open, checking the time. "It should be dark outside. If we're going to try it, now is the time."

"We've been in here that long?" Jack was surprised.

Angie nodded.

"You know what they say," Marcel muttered. "Time flies when you're having fun."

Jack smiled. "Does that mean you changed your mind? You coming with us?"

"I was outvoted, wasn't I? Either way, you guys are gonna open that door. I'm not staying here by myself. There's safety in numbers. Besides, my head hurts. Think I'm probably dehydrated, so I need to find some water, at the very least. Either that, or start licking the ice off those boxes over there."

They fell silent. Sammi, Angie and Marcel stared at Jack, waiting for him to make a decision. It was not lost on him that somehow, he'd become their leader. He swallowed hard and took a deep breath.

"We need weapons, just in case they are waiting for us." He reached into his jacket pocket and pulled out a box cutter. "Look around. What do we have?"

They searched the freezer, hunting through the shelves, racks and drawers, and looking under pallets. Marcel found a jagged length of wood from a broken skid. A nail jutted from the end. He swung the board through the air, testing it.

"That'll work for me."

Sammi found an old mop and broke the handle over her knee, creating a makeshift spear. She winced in pain, and rubbed her knee. Although he didn't say it out loud, Jack was impressed. Sure, Sammi had muscles from her particular type of bulimia, but he was surprised she had enough strength to snap the handle. Maybe her fear was giving her extra power.

Then he noticed that she was also rubbing her wrist.

"You okay?"

She nodded, grimacing. "Yeah. Jeremy almost broke my wrist earlier. It's just a little sore."

Angie grabbed a pack of frozen steaks.

"What are you gonna do with those?" Sammi asked.

Angie smacked the steaks against her thigh with a loud whack. She grinned. "Knock somebody out until I find something better."

Sammi returned the smile. "That's pretty kick ass.

"I thought so, too."

Jack extended the blade of his box-cutter. The dim overhead bulb glinted off the razor's edge. He took a deep breath and shuddered.

"I hope I don't have to use this. I've never . . . cut anybody before."

"Maybe they're gone," Sammi said. "It's pretty quiet out there now."

Nodding, Jack looked at each of them. They nodded back in return.

"Okay," he said, "let's do it."

"You guys sure about this?" Marcel whispered. "Maybe we should wait?"

Jack frowned. "I thought you were coming with us?"

"I am. But I've never been more fucking scared in my life. Just stalling I guess."

"We're all scared," Angie said. "But if we wait any longer, we'll freeze to death. Let's get it over with, before we lose our nerve."

They surrounded the door, weapons at the ready. Their breath clouded the air. Working as quietly as he could, Jack sliced through the strapping bands and shrink-wrap . Then, with one last glance at the others, he opened the door. It swung slowly outward. Jack's breath caught in his chest. He shielded his eyes with his free hand. Behind him, the others did the same. The lights were still on in the stockroom, and they were temporarily blinded by the brightness.

Sammi sniffed. "What's that smell?"

Their eyes slowly adjusted to the light. Angie gasped, dropping her steak. It thumped on the floor. Marcel retched.

Turning away, Sammi put her hand over her mouth and nose. Jack stepped out into the wreckage and tried to be brave. His left shoe squelched on something—a kidney, a liver, a spleen—he wasn't sure what. Some kind of internal organ. That much he could confirm. When he picked up his foot, there was a tread mark in the remains.

The stockroom had been ransacked. Blood-spattered boxes and cartons were ripped open. Some of the containers had been emptied of their original contents and were now filled with gore. Cases of canned goods had been dumped out on the floor. A stack of skids had fallen over. Arms and legs stuck out from beneath the wooden pallets. Blood pooled around an upended pallet jack. The lower half of a naked torso lay on the floor. Innards stretched away from the body like fleeing snakes. A dead man hung from a forklift, the prongs impaling his limp corpse. Severed hands, limbs, fingers and heads lay everywhere, along with unidentifiable scraps of human tissue—cuts of meat that mirrored the choices in the butcher's showcase up front. The room was silent, except for the incessant buzzing of flies. It stank—blood, shit, slaughter. The unpainted concrete walls were red. So was the floor. Blood had even splattered across the ceiling.

"Well," Angie said, "the power's still on."

Marcel gagged. "I wish it wasn't."

Jack tried to respond and found that he couldn't. He just reeled instead. The stockroom seemed to spin and his vision blurred. He knelt on the floor, leaned over, and vomited. Marcel did the same a moment later. Sammi and Angie stood guard until they recovered, looking around nervously. The room remained deserted. Both men slowly rose, unsteady, wiping their mouths.

"You okay?" Jack rasped.

"Yeah," Marcel said. "I will be. Getting a killer headache, though. Probably from all this stress."

"Might be dehydration," Angie said. "Like you said before."

"Or stress," Sammi offered. "Tension. Maybe you should rest."

Marcel shrugged. "Don't worry about me. I'm all right."

Jack turned to Sammi and Angie. His cheeks turned red with embarrassment. "Sorry about doing that in front of you."

"Don't worry about it," Angie said. "Happens to everybody. If it makes you any happier, I feel like puking, too."

Sammi giggled. "Nice to see somebody other than me throwing up for once."

"Girls rule," Angie whispered, "and boys drool."

Marcel scowled at the comment, flicking a thread of saliva from his chin.

"You sure you're all right?" Jack asked him.

Marcel nodded. His expression was one of annoyance.

"You girls ready?" Jack asked.

"Yes," Sammi whispered. "Let's quit stalling. The smell is getting worse back here."

"Okay," Jack whispered. "Let's see what is what."

He led them forward, trying not to look at the carnage, trying not to hear the sounds their shoes made as they stepped through a glistening tangle of stripped flesh or intestine, or the slow drips of blood falling from the stains on the ceiling. Jack wondered how the blood had gotten up there. He could read nothing in the splash patterns. They were everywhere—a crisscross of crimson.

At the end of the warehouse was an employee restroom. The door was slightly ajar. Although it was dark inside, they could make out the form of a woman crouched in front of the toilet. The seat was up. Her shoulders rested on the rim. Her head was deep inside the bowl. Water dripped from the faucet, and the mirror on the wall was shattered. The edges of the white porcelain sink were splashed with red, just like everything else in the warehouse. A sign on the wall next to the bathroom admonished all employees to wash their hands before returning to work. The irony filled Jack with a sick sense of dread.

He turned back to the others. "So far, so good."

"Maybe they're all dead," Sammi whispered.

"Let's hope so. Just stay quiet and stick together. Okay?"

Angie and Sammi nodded in understanding. Marcel

appeared distracted. His eyes were shut and his expression was pained. One hand clutched the length of wood. The other rubbed his right temple, fingers probing deep into the flesh.

"Marcel?" Jack reached for him. "What's the matter? I know you said you were okay, but you don't look so hot."

The older man glanced up at them. His eyes were red and watery. When he spoke, he sounded tired.

"What's up?" he rasped. "Sorry, I wasn't paying attention. What did you ask?"

"What's wrong with you, dude?"

"My fucking head hurts. That's all. I think Sammi's right. It's just the stress. Exhaustion. Just need to get some painkillers."

"You okay to keep going?" Jack asked. "We can stop if you need to."

Marcel nodded. "Yeah, I'll be fine. Lead on, kemosabe."

"Kemo-what?"

Marcel frowned. "You never saw The Lone Ranger?"

"No," Jack said. "I think my grandfather used to watch it when he was a kid."

"Never mind."

They approached the large double doors that led out into the grocery store. Jack and Angie peeked through the windows, while Sammi and Marcel hung back.

"Holy shit," Jack moaned.

FOUR

The slaughter in the stockroom paled in comparison to what awaited them in the store. They smelled the carnage even through the closed doors—a noxious brew of blood, piss, shit, bleach, ammonia, and other chemicals from the household cleaning products aisle. The stench made their eyes water and their throats and sinuses burn.

"I don't see anybody moving," Angie whispered after a moment. "Maybe they all left. I say we make a run for it."

"What do you guys think?" Jack asked Sammi and Marcel without turning around.

A loud crack rang out behind them. Sammi breathed a long, drawn-out sigh. Marcel laughed—a bubbling, high-pitched croak.

Jack and Angie turned around. Sammi stared at them, her head cocked to the right, her eyes glassy. A thin ribbon of blood trickled down the side of her face. Marcel stood behind her, gripping his club with both hands. The other end—the piece with the nail in it—was embedded in the top of Sammi's skull. The mop-handle spear slipped from Sammi's fingers. Her knees buckled. Marcel released the weapon and Sammi toppled to the floor. She thrashed on her side, arms and legs jittering, mouth agape.

"Fuck!" The razor knife shook in Jack's trembling hands.

"She was stealing from me," Marcel explained, his voice calm and self-assured. "She was stealing my thoughts. I had to teach her a lesson. Had to curb that shit."

"Sammi?" Jack whispered, hoping she'd respond. Her convulsions grew weaker.

"You guys would have done the same thing," Marcel said. "She was inside my head, stealing everything I thought about. If you're taking her side, then I have to assume you were stealing from me, too. And that means I'll have—"

Angie's scream cut him off. "You son of a bitch!"

She lunged at him, swinging the pack of steaks. The frozen meat collided with Marcel's head, stunning him. Jack heard the crack, even over Angie's cries. Marcel's head

41

rocked backward. Grunting, he staggered to the side. Already his ear had begun to swell. Before he could recover, Angie hit him again, breaking his nose and driving the splintered cartilage up into his brain. Marcel made a gulping noise. His eyes fluttered and his hands clenched, then unclenched. A single tear slid down his cheek. He fell forward, his body jittering on the floor next to Sammi. As they watched, Sammi's movements ceased and Marcel's slowed. A dark stain spread across his pants. The sharp smell of urine filled the air, mixing with the store's miasma.

"He's still alive," Jack said, watching him flop around.

"No he's not." Angie dropped the steaks and checked Marcel's pulse. "He's dead."

"But he's moving. And he pissed himself. Look at him."

"That's just the last few electrical impulses from his brain. It will stop in a minute."

Even as she said it, the convulsions slowed more, just as Sammi's had. Marcel's limbs twitched a few more times, and then ceased. Jack watched with a mixture of awe and revulsion.

"How did you know how to do that?"

Angie shrugged. "I didn't. My grandfather was in Vietnam. He served in the First Cavalry and went through all that hand-to-hand combat training. He told me once that if you hit somebody in the nose just right—and hard enough—it would kill them. I was never sure about it until now, though. Guess he was right."

"Jesus . . ."

Angie knelt by Sammi and felt her throat, checking her pulse as well. Jack watched with trepidation.

"Is she?"

Angie nodded. "Yes. She's dead. Poor kid."

"Damn."

"Were you friends?"

"Not really. I mean, we knew each other. But that was all. She dated a friend of mine for a little while."

"Yeah. I kind of got that impression while listening to you talk in the freezer."

Jack tried to swallow. His throat felt tight, his breathing constricted.

Angie picked up Sammi's spear. "You okay, Jack?"

"Yeah. I just . . . I've never seen anything happen like that before. Never saw somebody die."

"Neither have I, until today."

"It's not like in the movies, is it?"

"No," she agreed, "it's not. Not at all. But we'd both better get used to it. I've got a feeling that's the new world order."

"What do you mean?"

"I think you were right. Your theory—the magic beans? The beanstalk?"

"Seriously?"

Angie shrugged. "Why not, Jack? I mean, shit, it's not like I've got any better ideas. None of this makes any sense."

"But if the Prozac protected us, then why did Marcel snap like that?"

"He said he'd missed a dose. Maybe that was all it took. One missed dosage and you go nuts like everybody else. Perhaps it just took a while to catch up with him. Maybe the Prozac had to leave his system first."

Jack glanced back out at the store. "If that's the case, then we'd better stock up on meds before we leave. God knows when we'll find some again."

Angie leaned against the wall and sighed. She closed her eyes. Her body shook slightly.

"You cold?"

She shook her head, sliding down the wall until she crouched.

"Depressed?"

"No. Yes. Look . . . Jack—I'm not a commando. I've never killed anybody before. Just give me a few minutes, okay?"

"Sure." He turned back to the window, granting her some privacy. "I'll keep watch until you're ready."

"Thanks. I appreciate it."

Jack looked out the smudged glass, staring at the carnage. From his vantage point, he had a view of the freezer aisles and part of the dairy aisle. He knew them well. He worked them several nights a week and most weekends—rotating

43

the milk, yogurt, and sour cream; restocking frozen pizzas and vegetables, TV dinners, ice cream and a hundred other items. He barely recognized the aisles now. The glass doors in the frozen vegetables section were shattered. Mist curled out of the freezer, lazily rising towards the ceiling. Dead bodies littered the floor, sometimes three high. The few areas without corpses were littered with pieces of them. Blood and scarlet handprints covered the other freezer doors. Somebody had removed the popsicles from their shelves and replaced them with dozens of severed heads—men, women, and children, young and old.

People-sicles, Jack thought.

He stifled a laugh. It scared him. Was he cracking up, too? Would he be turning on Angie next? He didn't feel crazy, but would he really know if the illness was starting to set in? All his life, he'd had to deal with people picking on him about his mental illness. Cruel taunts and jokes from classmates who had no fucking clue. He'd been called crazy a thousand times, but now . . .

He glanced over his shoulder at Angie. Her eyes were still closed, her face serene.

No, he decided that he wasn't crazy. He was just scared. They both were.

He heard movement behind him. Jack turned, and saw Angie climbing slowly to her feet.

"You ready?" she asked.

He nodded. "Ready if you are."

Angie made a seesaw motion with her hand. "Not, really. But I sure as hell don't want to stay here."

They crept into the store. The double doors creaked on their hinges. Jack had never noticed them doing it before, but now, the sound seemed to echo down the aisles. Both of them braced for an attack, but the store appeared deserted. Muzak still played over the loudspeakers—Elton John's 'Island Girl'. Even though he hated the song, Jack knew all the words. It always came on at least once during his shifts. It used to be an annoyance. Now, the song filled him with dread—and a strange, surreal sense of longing. It was familiar in a world that was anything but. It reminded him of home.

Home. The word ran through his head, looking for something to connect with. His parents—he hadn't thought of them since this whole thing began. Were they okay? Both of them worked during the day. Chances were good they'd been sitting in rush hour traffic when everything happened. Depending on how far the illness had spread, they could be okay. Maybe they were out of range.

And maybe not.

Elton John continued wailing. *"You feel her nail scratch your back just like a rake. He one more gone, he one more John, who make the mistake."*

Jack shivered.

"That music's creepy," Angie whispered, echoing his thoughts.

"Yeah, it is."

"Why don't grocery stores play stuff like the Foo Fighters or Dave Matthews or The Mighty Mighty Bosstones?"

"I don't know." He shrugged. "It could be worse."

"What could possibly be any worse than Elton John?"

"Fergie. The Pussycat Dolls. Fall Out Boy. Kanye West. Take your pick."

"You fight dirty, Jack."

He grinned, despite his fears. "So do you."

She reached out and took his hand, giving it a squeeze. Jack squeezed back.

"Don't get the wrong idea," Angie said. "This doesn't mean we're gonna hook up. You're a little too young for me."

"Okay . . ."

"This is just because I'm happy to be alive and because I'm scared. Understand?"

"No worries," Jack said, trying to project confidence. "Don't be scared. I'll protect you. My doctor didn't call me Jack the Giant-Killer for nothing."

"You'll protect me? So far, I've been covering your ass."

"I know," Jack admitted. "But I was hoping you wouldn't notice."

Despite their efforts to stay quiet, both of them giggled. Then they moved on, still holding hands. They moved

45

slowly, picking their way around human wreckage. Angie slipped in a pile of intestines. Jack accidentally dropped his knife and bumped into a bloody shopping cart full of severed feet—most of them still wearing shoes. Elton John gave way to Christopher Cross, singing about being lost between the moon and New York City. Jack and Angie knew how he felt.

"Notice something?" Angie asked.

"What's that?"

"I think we're alone in here. They're all dead. Each and every last one of them. It's like they butchered each other until there was nothing left."

"Well, we should still be careful. Somebody had to be the last one standing. He or she might still be around. Or there may be others like Marcel, that didn't change until now."

What he thought to himself but didn't say out loud was that they should probably be wary of each other, too.

They made it to the pharmacy without encountering trouble. Angie paled as they approached the counter. Her grip tightened around Jack's hand.

"What's wrong?" he whispered. "Did you hear something?"

"No," she said. "Just brings back bad memories."

"Well, wait here. I'll try to hurry."

"Where are you going?"

"To get us some meds. If my theory is right, then we're gonna need them."

"Did you ever work in a pharmacy?"

"No."

"Then how the hell do you know what you're looking for?"

"Prozac is really fluoxotine, so that's what they should have it labeled as."

The pharmacy's employee door was locked. Setting his box-cutter aside, Jack vaulted over the counter. There were two corpses behind it. One of them, a woman, was missing her eyes. The other, a man, lay on his stomach. His head had been bashed in with a coffee maker. Jack knew because the bloody appliance lay next to the corpse.

"Is it bad?" Angie called.

"Not as bad as out there, but it ain't pretty either."

He stepped over the bodies and went to the back. Then he searched through the shelves and bins until he found what he was looking for—a drawer full of fluoxotine.

"Bingo!"

"You found some?"

"Yep. Grab me a bag, will you?"

"Paper or plastic?"

"Plastic. Easier to carry."

Angie retrieved a plastic bag from one of the registers and handed it to him over the counter. Jack returned to the shelf, yanked the drawer out of the cabinet, and dumped its contents into the bag. Then he returned to the counter and smiled.

"Do you have your insurance card with you?"

Angie gave him a puzzled look. "No. Why?"

"Oh, well." Jack chuckled nervously. "What the hell. Prozac's on the house today. Can I interest you in some free samples of Oxy-Contin, as well? Or how about some high-grade pharmaceutical marijuana?"

"Just the anti-depressants, please. Thanks."

"Angie . . ." Jack shook his head. "You should never turn down free weed."

"We should probably divide up the meds," Angie suggested. "In case we get separated or something."

"Okay," Jack agreed, "but I think we should take them at the same time. That way, we can sort of remind each other. Less chance of forgetting a dose."

"Good idea."

"Thanks."

"So what now?" Angie asked. "Do you think we should leave?"

"That depends. You've probably got people you want to check on. So do I. We need to at least determine if the whole city is like this. The power is still on. Maybe we can find a television or a radio—check the news and see if we can learn anything."

"Something tells me we're not going to."

"That's crazy talk," Jack teased.

"I just think we just need to prepare for the worst possible scenario. You and I might very well be the only two sane people left in this city. What if we find our loved ones and they're like everybody else? Or what if they're still alive—and they try to kill us? Could you defend yourself against your family? Do you have what it takes to stay alive? To kill them?"

Jack's expression soured. "I don't want to think about it."

"You might not have a choice, Jack."

"Shit . . ."

"And there's something else to consider."

"What?"

"While we're watching each other's backs, we also need to keep an eye on each other. If either of us misses a dose—or if we're wrong about that and this . . . whatever it was that caused this, infects one of us, the other could be in real danger."

"We'll be okay," Jack insisted. "In truth, I was thinking about that earlier. I figure that if we were gonna go psycho, we would have changed when Marcel did."

"We don't know that. We don't know anything."

Jack's expression fell. "So you think we should split up? Go our separate ways?"

"No. I just think we should be careful around each other. Marcel was complaining about a headache right before he snapped. If either of us gets a headache, we should tell each other right away. Agreed?"

"And then what? We kill the person with the headache? We abandon them?"

"I don't know."

Jack sighed. He looked as if he were ready to cry.

"Look," Angie said after a pause, "I think you're right about finding some news. Let's try that first. We'll worry about everything else in time."

"Okay."

Still using caution, they found two student-sized backpacks in the employee locker room. They filled these with bottles of spring water, crackers, sardines, dried fruit, and other canned goods, as well as medical supplies, toiletries, matches, cigarette lighters, and anything else that might prove useful. Jack considered grabbing some cash from the registers, but decided against it. He wasn't sure what good cash would do them now, except to maybe start a fire with. Angie took a carton of cigarettes from behind the customer service counter.

"Do you smoke?"

She shook her head and then shrugged. "Fuck it. I do now."

They crept to the front of the store. The electronic eyes above the doors registered their movements and the doors slid open as they approached.

"Oh . . ." Angie stared out at the parking lot. Sodium lights bathed it in a sickly yellow glow. "It's even worse than it is in here."

Jack said nothing.

FIVE

The parking lot was littered with corpses and debris. Something had sparked a fire, and many of the cars were now nothing more than blackened hulls. Some of the bodies were burned as well. Crows and other birds perched on the dead, scavenging the choice bits. The stench was revolting. A dog wandered amidst the chaos, but ran away when it saw them.

Slowly, they walked outside, clutching their weapons, supplies, and most importantly, Jack's magic beans. The doors slid shut behind them, and the electricity went out, plunging the store and the parking lot into total darkness. Squawking, the birds took flight. The stench grew stronger.

"I can't see shit," Angie whispered.

"Neither can I. The power must be out everywhere."

Jack looked around. There were no streetlights or glows from the windows of the nearby buildings. No car headlights, no radios blaring. Even the birds had fallen silent. He gazed up at the sky. The stars were hidden behind a curtain of clouds. He searched for the twinkling lights of a passing airplane, but the sky was empty.

The silence overwhelmed them.

"It's the end of the world," Jack said. "For real. The end of the fucking world."

"No," Angie disagreed. "It's not the end of the world. It's just the end of the people. The world will be just fine. Look around us. The world is still here. It's just the people that are gone."

"We can't be the only ones left alive," Jack said. "It doesn't make any sense. There has to be others like us."

To Angie, it sounded like he was trying to convince himself.

They took a few hesitant steps forward. Jack stumbled over a severed arm and almost tripped. After he regained his balance, Angie found his hand in the dark and held on tight.

"Be careful," she whispered. "Wouldn't do to break your leg after all of this."

"That would suck. Doctors might be hard to come by now."

50

She held up a hand, silencing him. Her expression was alarmed.

"What's wrong?" Jack whispered.

Angie nodded at the Chinese restaurant, adjoined to the supermarket. The door was slightly ajar. The smell of cooking meat drifted out of the building. Despite his terror, Jack's mouth watered.

"Listen," Angie mouthed.

Jack cocked his head and focused. After a moment, he heard it—a slight rustling sound, followed by a crunching noise. Someone walking on broken glass, perhaps, and trying to be stealthy about it.

Gripping her weapon tightly, Angie crept toward the open door.

Something zipped by them—an angry bee. A second later, they heard the shot.

"Get down," Jack shouted.

Angie was already ahead of him. She flung herself to the pavement, skinning her elbows and knees. Another blast boomed across the parking lot. Ducking behind a toppled shopping cart, Jack saw a brief flash of light from inside the restaurant.

"Get out of here," a man screamed. "Get the fuck away from me, you crazy bastards!"

Unable to seek cover without becoming a target, Angie cast a terrified glance at Jack. Still cowering behind the shopping cart, he motioned at her to stay down.

"Hey," he shouted. "Stop shooting! We don't want to hurt you. We're not like the others!"

The unseen man responded by firing another round. A car windshield exploded nearby. Fragments of glass rained down on the pavement. When the echoes of the gunshot finally died down, they heard the shooter yelling.

"The whole fucking world's gone insane. But you won't get me!"

"We're not trying to," Jack insisted. "Nobody's going to hurt you. We just want to go home. Please!"

"Bullshit! You're like everybody else. Bug-fuck crazy. They were cooking people in here. *Cooking people who*

51

were still alive. Look at this grill! Who would do something like this?"

"Are you okay?" Jack called. "Are you injured? Do you need help?"

"You're trying to trick me. I let you come in, and you'll kill me. You think I was born yesterday, you crazy fucker?"

"We're not crazy," Angie yelled. "We're like you. We just escaped from the grocery store."

Jack decided to try a different tactic. "My name's Jack. This is Angie. What's your name?"

"Fuck you, Jack!"

"Why did you tell him our names?" Angie whispered.

"I'm trying to calm him down."

"Well, I don't want him knowing who I am. He just tried to kill us. Did it ever occur to you that he could be one of them? Maybe he's trying to lure us in?"

"He just said the same thing about us, Angie."

"That doesn't prove anything."

"Get out of here," the man hollered. "I'm not telling you again. If you don't leave right the fuck now, I'll drop you right there."

Jack cupped his hands over his mouth. "Are you on Prozac?"

The man didn't reply.

"If you are," Jack shouted, "then you need to keep taking it. You'll be okay as long as you stay medicated. We're leaving now. We don't want any trouble. Okay?"

Silence.

"Are you listening? Don't shoot us, man!"

Slowly, excruciatingly, Angie crawled towards Jack. She held her breath, anticipating another shot, expecting to feel a bullet slam into her—but the man in the restaurant had fallen silent. When she reached Jack, the two of them crab-walked to a nearby vehicle. They ducked down behind it, breathing hard.

"Well," Angie panted, "there's one crazy person who's not dead yet."

"I still don't think so." Jack wiped the sweat from his forehead with his t-shirt. "I don't think he was crazy."

"He tried to kill us!"

"Because he was afraid. And I think that's all it was. He's like us—he's scared. Paranoid."

"And that's what we've got to look forward to? Paranoia? Shooting at everyone, be they friend or foe?"

"Only if we give in to it."

He got quiet. His head hung low and his shoulders slumped. At first, Angie thought he was just waiting to see if the man in the restaurant had forgotten about them. The she realized he was sulking.

"What's wrong?" Angie asked.

"I've been thinking," Jack said. "When we get to a safer location, we need to check the expiration date on these pills."

"They won't have any," Angie reminded him. "We filled the prescription ourselves. We didn't print out one of those little labels that has the expiration date. But usually, I think it's about a year."

"Well, after we check on our families, our next stop *needs* to be another pharmacy, so we can load up on more."

Angie sighed. "So that's our life now? We're going to be drugstore cowboys, spending every day looking for more and more magic beans?"

"As fucked up as it is, yes. We need Prozac even more than we need food and water. Without Prozac, we're screwed. I mean, without it, we might as well just give up right now and march back there and let that guy shoot us. We need more."

"No," Angie said. "What we need is a fucking pharmacist. With no labs producing it, how long before we run out of magic beans?"

"One step at a time, my fellow giant-killer. One step at a time."

They slowly crossed the parking lot, taking deliberate steps and picking their way through the wreckage. Then they walked down the main drag, heading away from the relative safety of the store. Both of them felt eyes upon them, but when they glanced behind, there was no sign of the man with the gun.

The city skyline loomed in the distance. Columns of smoke rose into the sky. Massive fires burning on the freeway, washing the bellies of the clouds in a wavering orange glow. They saw signs of an explosion. The burned out shell of a tanker trunk sat smoldering on the median strip. The overpass had collapsed, burying the road beneath it in a mountainous pile of rubble. Chunks of concrete lay on top of crushed cars.

They reached an intersection and came across the first dead body. Then another. Then a dozen. Then two dozen. And then hundreds. Their revulsion grew with each city block. The streets resembled the grocery store's interior, but on a grander and more gruesome scale. The only thing moving were the birds—crows, gulls, pigeons; they swooped down from the rooftops, perching on the mounds of corpses and feasting on the choicest morsels. Dogs and cats and even a few rats were present as well, not quite as bold as the birds— but they would be by the time the sun went down.

Jack and Angie walked in silence. They stopped at a restaurant and grabbed some napkins, and then stuck the napkins in their noses to block out the smell. It was already bad. It would be unbearable after the corpses had laid out in the sun for a few days. After a while, the silence began to get to them both. Jack tried calling out once, but the sound of his voice echoing through the empty streets disturbed him even more than the carnage all around them.

"Jack?"

"What?"

"Are you sure we won't change?" Angie asked. "Are you sure we won't become like them?"

"Yes," Jack lied. "As long as we take our meds, we should be fine."

They went out into the world, and hoped they wouldn't wake the sleeping giant.

AFTERWORD

Jack's Magic Beans started with the opening sentence.

Okay. Yes, I know that's how all stories start, but in this case, that's all I had—the opening sentence. I had no ideas about plot or characters or even a title. All I had was an opening sentence. I typed: *The lettuce started talking to Ben Mahoney halfway through his shift at Save-A-Lot.* Then I stared at the laptop. I had no idea what happened next. I had no idea who Ben Mahoney was or why the lettuce was speaking to him.

About six months later, my wife at the time (now ex-wife but we remain best friends), Cassandra, told me about a business associate who referred to Prozac as 'magic beans'. I thought that was interesting. I mulled it over for an evening.

The next day, I knew what happened after the lettuce started talking.

What happened was this story.

I seem to write two kinds of stories. There are my serious books (such as *The Girl on the Glider, Ghoul, Dark Hollow*) and then there are my fun books (such as *The Conqueror Worms* and all of my zombie novels). Critics and fans may disagree with those classifications, but that's okay. These are just personal terms. This is how I think of my work. Anyway, I've noticed that I tend to write a fun book immediately after finishing a serious one. With the exception of the opening sentence, I wrote *Jack's Magic Beans* right after finishing *Ghoul*—and *Ghoul* was a novel that kicked my fucking ass on both a psychological and emotional level. It was a serious book. It was a hard book. It was probably—at that time—my most autobiographical work to date, and it was difficult to revisit some of the shit from my childhood and work it into my fiction. In short, it left me depressed.

Luckily, *Jack's Magic Beans* worked like an anti-depressant—just like in the story. Writing this novella was a cure for the depression I felt after battling my way through *Ghoul*.

Jack's Magic Beans was originally supposed to be

published by a small press. They never managed to get it into print (although they did publish a handful of promotional soft cover copies—I've never understood why they spent their money on promotional copies rather than just spending the same amount and publishing the actual book). When the contract expired and the book still wasn't published, I got my rights back. Then I included the novella as the opening story in my now out-of-print short story collection *Unhappy Endings*. And now, Deadite Press have brought it back into print for everyone to enjoy. And that is my hope. That you enjoyed it, and enjoy my other books, as well. You keep reading them and I'll keep writing them.

Brian Keene
January 2011

WITHOUT YOU

I woke up this morning and shot myself twice.

Carolyn had already left for work. She'd tried waking me repeatedly, as she does every morning. It's a game that has become an annoying ritual, much like the rest of my life.

The alarm went off for the first time at six. Like always, she was pressed up against me, and my morning hard on was wedged into her fat ass. She thinks that I still find her desirable, not realizing that every man in the world wakes up like that if he has a full bladder. Carolyn hasn't turned me on in over ten years.

She lay there, as she does every morning, with the alarm blaring, snuggling tighter against me until I wanted to scream. Her breath stank. Her hair stank. She stank. I always shower before bed, as well as in the morning. She only showers in the morning.

I reached over her and hit the snooze button. Ten minutes later the scene replayed itself. This time she got up and stumbled off to the bathroom. Drifting in and out of sleep, I heard her singing along with Britney Spears on the radio. That's something else that annoyed me. Here we were, both in our thirties, and she still insisted on listening to teenybopper pop music. I listened to talk radio mostly, but not Carolyn. She'd sing along with all that hip-hop shit.

It was enough to drive a man crazy.

After the shower, she walked into the bedroom, humming and dripping and babbling baby talk to me.

"Come on, my widdle poozie woozie, wakey wakey."

I groaned, wanting to die right then and there.

"Did I tire you out last night," she asked, as she ironed a skirt for work. "Am I too much for you?"

I mumbled an incoherent response, shuddering at thoughts of the previous evening's acrobatics. She'd come three times. I had to envision my mother just to get it up, and still I had to fake an orgasm. Thank God for rubbers.

Twenty minutes later, I was still lying there and Carolyn was more insistent, warning me that I'd be late for work. I told her I was sick, and her smothering concern made me want to leap out of my skin. Thankfully, she'd been late for work, and I got off lucky with only a quick kiss and a promise to call me during her lunch break.

I heard the door shut. A minute later, I heard the Saturn cough to life. The Saturn that we still owed over six grand on, even though it was a piece of shit. The Saturn that we'd just *had* to have, because that's what everybody else was driving. My S.U.V. had been bought for the same reason and we owed even more on it.

I rolled out of bed, walking through the house that we would be in debt for until our Sixties. I called into work, biting my lip to keep from arguing with Clarence when he questioned me. Twelve years I'd busted my ass for him. Twelve years of endless monotony, of heat and grime and boredom. Twelve years of ten-hour days with mandatory overtime, running a machine I was fated to operate until the soft haze of retirement. And after all of that, he had the fucking gall to suggest I was faking my illness?

My denial was short and terse. I hadn't meant to call Clarence a fat bastard until it slipped through my clenched teeth.

After he fired me, I slammed the phone down into the cradle. Something warm dribbled down my chin. I tasted blood. I'd bitten through my lower lip. Wincing, I stumbled into the bathroom and watched the blood drip from my chin. One drop landed on my white undershirt. My stomach, bloated from too much cheap beer, seemed to take up most of my reflection. Two days worth of stubble covered my face. There were dark shadows under my eyes. Lines had formed in the past year.

I tore a wad of toilet paper from the dispenser and balled it against my lip. With my free hand, I fingered the growth on my face, trying to decide if it was worth my time to shave. Gray hair peppered my goatee.

The first tear took me by surprise.

I was thirty-five going on seventy. I owed a mountain of debt and had just lost my job. I was married to a woman who I hadn't been in love with since shortly after high school. I had an ulcer, acid reflux, a receding hairline, and a bloody hole in my lip. My only friends were the other guys from work, and they were only my friends when I was buying the first round. I smoked two packs of cigarettes a day and dipped half a can of Skoal. Even now, a tumor was probably spiraling its way through my body.

More tears followed. I collapsed next to the toilet bowl, sobbing. Where had it all gone wrong? Carolyn and I had been so happy during our senior year. I had a terrific arm in football and a promising scholarship. The world was mine and I was God. I used to tremble after our lovemaking, which is what it was back then, not the obscene pantomime it had become now. I had loved her so much.

"Do you love me," she used to ask me afterward. "Do you really love me?"

I always replied, "I'd die without you."

Then Carolyn got pregnant halfway through our senior year and I kissed college goodbye. The baby was stillborn. We never tried again. I guess that was when I began the downward spiral.

The phone rang. I rose unsteadily, leaning on the sink for support. My head throbbed. The phone rang again, more insistent this time. It reminded me of Carolyn.

I gripped the receiver so hard that my knuckles turned white. Probably Clarence, calling back to berate me some more.

"Hello?"

There was a pause and a series of mechanical clicks. Then a female spoke, offering me a free appraisal for storm windows on the home I couldn't afford.

"I'm not interested," I said. "Put us on your do not call list."

"Can I axe you why, sir?" It sounded like she was reading from a script.

"You can't 'axe' me anything. You can 'ask' me if you'd like, but the answer is still fuck off!"

The telemarketer launched into a tirade then and I ripped the phone from the wall. I flung it across the room. It smashed into a lamp that Carolyn's mother had given to us for our fifth wedding anniversary. I stared at the fragments, felt fresh blood running down my chin again, and sighed.

I'd been contemplating it for weeks, but it wasn't until then that I decided to die.

I went to the gun cabinet. Inside were my hunting rifles,

kept for a pastime that I didn't enjoy, but that I had to partake in to be considered a normal guy. My hand was steady as I unlocked the case and selected the 30.06 and a box of shells. The bullets slid into the chamber with satisfying clicks. I sat down on the bed with the gun between my legs.

I had seen pictures online of failed suicide attempts. Cases where the poor slob had placed the gun against the side of his head and pulled the trigger, writhing in agony when the bullet traveled around his brain and left him alive. That was no good. I needed to do this the right way. I placed the barrel in my mouth, tasting the oil on the cold metal. I breathed through my nose, deep-throating the gun the way I'd done my Uncle's shriveled pecker when I was nine. As the barrel touched the back of my throat, I gagged, just like back then. Tears streamed down my face.

I glanced at the wedding picture on the nightstand. There was me and Carolyn. Two smiling people. Happy. In love. Not the balding loser who sat here now or the fat cow the woman had turned into.

The woman who I had promised to love forever so long ago.

"I'd die without you," I mumbled around the barrel.

Then I pulled the trigger.

The initial force jerked me backward. The gun barrel impaled the roof of my mouth. I felt it blast open my head and heard the wet slap of my brains hitting the wall, turning the ivory flowered wallpaper crimson. Grey chunks of brain matter and eggshell splinters of my fragmented skull embedded themselves in the drywall. My right eye dribbled down my face as my bladder and sphincter let loose, staining the bed sheets.

The pain stopped abruptly, as if someone had flicked a light switch. One moment I was writhing in agony and trying to scream around the gun. Then there was nothing.

But I was conscious.

I wasn't dead. I'd fucked this up, too.

I pulled the trigger again. The second shot erased what was left of the top and back of my head. My face sagged down a few inches, making it hard to see clearly. Bits of skin and gristle dangled down my neck. The room stank of blood and shit and cordite.

The gunshots echoed throughout the house, drowning out my heavy breathing.

Letting the rifle slip from my numb fingers, I shuffled to the mirror and looked at the damage I'd inflicted. I had to shrug my shoulders a few times in order to get my face back up to eye level.

It wasn't pretty.

I should have been dead, yet there I stood. I reached behind me, letting my fingers play across the gaping hole where my brain had been. There was nothing. No bald spot, no scalp, no skull. Nothing.

The phone rang again. It sounded muffled, thanks to my one remaining ear. After four rings, the answering machine clicked on.

"Hi, honey." Carolyn. "I just wanted to see how you were feeling."

"My headache is gone." Laughing, I spat out a piece of myself. "I've cured the common headache."

"Anyway," she continued, "I've got to get back to work. See you when I get home. I love you."

"I'd die without you." My voice dripped with sarcasm.

Then it hit me—the reason that I was still alive.

So now I'm sitting here at the kitchen table, writing this while my insides dry on the bedroom wall. I'm almost free of this hell that is my life. Carolyn will be home soon, and I will fulfill the promise that I made to her so long ago.

The original version of this story appeared in my first short story collection, No Rest For the Wicked, *which is long out-of-print. Several years ago, I revised the story considerably for a collection called* A Little Silver Book of Streetwise Stories *(which is also now out-of-print). I've always liked the idea, but hated the writing in the original—it was the amateur work of an author still struggling to find his voice. I like this version much better and am happy to share it with you here. The story was inspired by a late-night conversation with an old friend.*

I AM
AN EXIT

I found him lying along the interstate, bleeding in the moonlight under the sign for Exit Five. It was bad—real bad. Blood covered everything; from the guard rail and median strip to his frayed blue jeans and crooked birth-control glasses with the cracked lens. They called them birth control glasses because wearing them insured that you'd never get laid. You only got glasses like that in the military and in prison. He didn't look like a soldier to me.

Far away, barely visible through the woods, an orange fire glowed. A hint of smoke drifted towards us on the breeze.

I knelt down beside him, and he struggled to sit up. His insides glistened, slipping from the wound in his side. Gently, I urged him back to the ground and then placed my hand over the gash, feeling the slick, wet heat beneath my palm. The wind buffeted the Exit Five sign above our heads, and then died.

"Don't try to sit up," I told him. "You're injured."

He tried to speak. His cracked lips were covered with froth. The words would not come. He closed his eyes.

With my free hand, I reached into the pocket of my coat, and he opened his eyes again, focusing on me. I pulled my hand back out, keeping the other one on the gash in his side.

"Robin."

"Sorry friend. Just me."

"I was—trying to get home to Robin."

He coughed, spraying blood and spittle, and I felt his innards move beneath my palm.

"She's waiting for me."

I nodded, not understanding but understanding all the same.

He focused on me again. "What happened?"

"You've been in an accident."

"I—I don't—last thing I remember was the fire."

"Sshhhhh."

He coughed again.

"My legs feel like they're asleep."

"Probably because you've been lying down," I lied. "They're okay."

They weren't. One was squashed flat in several places and bent at an angle. A shard of bone protruded from the other.

"D-do you have a cell phone? I want to call Robin."

"Sorry friend. Wish I did, so we could call 911. But I'm sure someone will come along. Meanwhile, tell me about her."

"She's beautiful." His grimace turned into a smile, and the pain and confusion vanished from his eyes. "She's waiting for me. Haven't seen her in five years."

"Why is that?"

"Been in prison." He swallowed. "Upstate. Cresson. Just got out this morning. Robbery. I stole a pack of cigarettes. Can you believe that shit? Five years for one lousy pack of smokes."

I shook my head. I'd been right about the glasses. And the sentence indicated he wasn't a first time offender. Pennsylvania had a three strikes law, and it sounded as if he qualified.

A mosquito buzzed in my ear, but I ignored it. In the distance, the fire grew brighter.

"We'd been dating before it happened," he said. "She was pregnant with my son. I—I've never held him."

"They didn't come visit you?"

"Not enough money. Cresson is a long way from Hanover—almost on the New York border. We didn't have no car."

He paused, struggling to sit up again. "My legs are cold."

"That's okay," I said. "The important thing is to keep talking. Tell me more."

"I—I got out this morning. Couldn't wait to get home and see her and the kid. Kurt. We named him Kurt, like the singer, you know? The guy from Nirvana? She wrote me letters every single day. I used to call her collect, but Robin still lives with her folks, and it got too expensive. I've s-seen pictures of Kurt. Watched him grow up through the mail. I want to hug him. My stomach is cold."

"It's a cold night," I replied, trying to take his mind off of it. He was losing a lot of blood. The smoke was stronger now, heavier. It blanketed the treetops and drifted over the road like fog.

"The State got me a Greyhound ticket from Cresson to Hanover. Rode on that damn bus all day, and I was tired, but I couldn't sleep. Too excited. There was a McDonalds at one of the stops, and that's the first time I've had a Quarter-Pounder in five years! Couldn't wait to tell Robin about it."

His eyes grew dark.

"There was this one fucker on the bus though. Guy from Cresson, just like me. Never saw him before. He was in a different block. He was on his way to Harrisburg. Fucker started the fight, but the bus driver didn't believe me and threw me off."

"Really?"

"Yeah!" He broke into a violent fit of coughing, and I thought that would be it, that he would expire. But then it subsided. "Fucker threw me right off the bus. Right here on the road. I had my thumb out to hitch a ride when I saw—*I saw the fire!*"

He sat upright, eyes startled.

"Shit, I r-remember now. There's a house on fire!"

"Yes," I soothed him, forcing him back down. "Yes, there is. But there's nothing you can do about that now. Somebody should be along shortly. What else do you remember?"

His eyes clouded.

"T-the fire—and then—a horn? A loud horn, like on a tractor-trailer, and bright lights."

"Hmmmm."

"Mister? I don't feel too good. I don't think I'm gonna make it. Will you d-do me a f-favor?"

I nodded. His skin felt cold; the warmth was leaving his body.

"Give my love to Robin and K-kurt? Their address is in m-my wallet, along w-with t-t-their phone number."

"I'd be happy too."

"I—I s-sure-a-a-appreciate t-that, Mister."

He smiled, safe in the knowledge that I would give his wife and child his love. Then he turned his head to the fire in the distance. His brow creased.

"I s-sure h-hope the p-people in that h-house are a-alright . . ."

"They are fine now," I told him. "There were four of them. Daddy, Mommy, and the kids, a boy and a girl. The Wilts, I believe their name was. Exit Four. I killed them long before I started the fire. So don't worry yourself. They'll never feel the flames."

"W-what?" He tried to sit up again, but I shoved him back down, hard.

"They were Exit Four. You are Exit Five. Hold still."

I pulled the knife from my jacket and cut his throat. There wasn't as much blood as I'd expected, most of it already having leaked out while I kept him talking. I wiped the knife in the grass and placed it back in my coat. Then I fished out his wallet and found Robin and Kurt's address and phone number. I smiled. They lived just off the Interstate, at Exit Twenty-One.

Twenty-One. And this was Five. Sixteen more exits, and I would keep my promise to him.

I walked on into the night, the distant wail of fire sirens following in my wake.

I am an exit.

Many readers tell me this story is one of their favorites. "I Am An Exit" appeared in my second short story collection, Fear of Gravity, *and was reprinted in* A Little Silver Book of Streetwise Stories. *Both of those collections are now out-of-print, and people who don't own them and don't want to pay an exorbitant amount of money for them on eBay keep asking me to reprint it, so here you go.*

The tale came in a single, sudden burst. I usually write to music. The night this was written, I was working on the first draft of a novel called Terminal, *and listening to Johnny Cash's "Give My Love To Rose" and Nine Inch Nails' "Mr. Self Destruct." When the story idea came, it was the perfect fusion of fatigue, music, coffee and creative energy. The lyrics from both songs kept running around in my head. I thought about Cash's protagonist dying along the railroad tracks, begging the stranger to give his love to Rose, while in the background, Trent Reznor whispered "I am an exit." I wrote the first draft in the next half hour, and the second and final drafts the following day.*

The story was so well-received that I eventually wrote a sequel to it (which follows).

THIS IS
NOT
AN EXIT

"You ever kill anyone?"

He licks his lips when he asks me, and I can tell by his expression that he doesn't really want to know. His eyes dart around the hotel bar before coming back to me. No matter what I say, my answer will barely register with him. The question is perfunctory. He desires the act of confession. He's killed, and it's eating at him. It weighs on him. He needs to tell.

"What?" I pretend to be shocked by the question.

The young man is maybe twenty-one or two. Still learning his limits when it comes to alcohol. His slurred words are barely noticeable, but the empty beer bottles in front of him reveal everything. He leans closer, nearly falling off his stool.

"Have you ever killed someone?"

This is his conversation starter. A chance to unburden. Or to brag. This is a beginning.

An entrance.

I close entrances.

The first person I ever killed was named Lawrence. I've killed so many people over the years that they blur together—a nameless, faceless conglomerate. But I remember Lawrence. Pale and pasty. Hair on his knuckles. Rheumy eyes. He drove a red Chrysler mini-van and the glove compartment was full of Steely Dan cassettes and porn. Lawrence cried when I cut the sigils into his skin. Mucous bubbled out of his nose and ran into his mouth. Disgusting back then, but oddly amusing now. It brings a smile to my face, like thoughts of a childhood friend or first love.

In the years since, I've streamlined my efforts. I no longer bother with sigils or ceremony. I no longer speak the words of closing. The mere act of killing accomplishes my work. Spilling blood closes the doors. I don't need the rest of the trappings. Indeed, I prefer to act quickly these days. A shot in the dark. A knife to the back. Burn them as they sleep. Over and done. No muss. No fuss. Move on up the highway to the next exit. There are miles to go and doors to close before I rest, and I am getting older. Robert Frost took the road less traveled, but I take all roads. Speed and efficiency are the key. I didn't know that, back when I killed Lawrence.

I know it now.

I am swift. My avatar is a hummingbird. Metaphorically speaking, I move through the night at eighty miles per second, traveling from blossom to blossom, taking their nectar and then moving on.

I tell the young man none of this. Instead, I say, "No, I've never killed anyone."

"I have. A few years ago."

I sip my scotch and dab my lips with the napkin. When I respond, I try not to sound disinterested.

"Really?"

"Yeah." He nods. "Seriously. I'm not bullshitting you."

I say nothing, waiting, hoping he'll unburden himself soon so that I can go to my room and sleep. Dawn is coming and I must be on my way.

He signals for another round. We sit in silence until the bartender brings our drinks. The man glances at my half-full glass of scotch and I smile. He sets the drinks down and helps another customer. The young man picks up his beer and drinks half the bottle. I watch his throat work. He puts the bottle down and wipes the condensation on his jeans.

"My girlfriend's name was Janey," he says. "I was eighteen. She was fourteen. I mean, that's only four year's difference, but people acted like I was a fucking child molester or something. I wasn't, dog. I knew Janey since we were little kids. Our parents took us to the same church and shit. We were in love. Her old man freaked when he found out we were doing it. Somehow—I don't know how—he got the password to Janey's MySpace page and he read our messages. He told her she wasn't allowed to see me anymore. Then he called my folks and said if I tried to contact Janey again, he'd call the cops and have me arrested as a pedophile. He actually called me that—like I was one of those sick fucks Chris Matthews busts on that show. You know?"

I don't. The only television programming I watch is PBS, and only when the hotel I'm staying in offers it. But I nod just the same, encouraging him to continue. I hope he'll hurry up. I am bored.

"Well, Janey sent me a text message the next day. Her dad found out and he smacked the shit out of her. So I went over there and knocked on the door, and when he answered, I told him I wanted to talk. He was mad. So mad that he was fucking shaking, yo. But he let me in. Said we were gonna have this out once and for all, and then he never wanted to see me again. He made Janey stay upstairs in her room. I heard her and her mother arguing. I asked if I could get a glass of water and he said yeah. So when he went into the kitchen to get it, I followed him. They must have just gone grocery shopping, because there were a bunch of empty plastic bags lying on the counter. I picked up two—double-bagged, like they do for heavy stuff, you know? There was a little bit of blood inside, probably from steak or hamburger or something. I remember that. And while her dad's back was still turned, I slipped those bags over his head and smothered the motherfucker."

There is no regret in his voice as he says this. There is only grim satisfaction. His smile is a death mask. He takes another sip of beer and then continues.

"Upstairs, Janey and her mom were still hollering at each other, so I grabbed a knife from the drawer and tip-toed out of the kitchen. Janey's little brother, Mikey, was standing there. He screamed, so I stabbed him, just to shut him up." He chuckles, but there is no humor in it. "Yeah, I shut him the fuck up, alright. I remember when I pulled the knife out, blood just started gushing. It was hot and sticky, you know?"

I do indeed. I know all too well what another's blood feels like on your hands. How it smells. How it steams on cold nights and turns black when spilled on asphalt. How it dries on your flesh like mud, and can be peeled away like dead skin.

I tell him none of this. Instead, I finish my scotch and reach for the second glass. I hold it in my hands, not drinking.

"How did that make you feel?" I ask.

He blinks, as if he'd forgotten I was there.

"W-what?"

"Killing your girlfriend's brother. How did you feel about it?"

He shrugs. "I don't know. I didn't really feel anything at the time, except maybe scared. Janey's mom heard him scream. By the time Mikey hit the floor, she was running down the stairs, hollering at Janey to call 911. So I chased her down and shut her ass up, too. I didn't really think about it. I just did it. The news said I stabbed her mom forty-seven times, but I didn't count."

I arch my eyebrows, bemused. Forty-seven is a powerful number. It has meaning in certain occult circles, but I doubt he is aware of the significance.

"I went into Janey's room. She was hiding in the closet. Crying and shit. I told her we could be together now. We could leave, before anybody figured out what had happened. Take her parents car and just fucking drive, dog. Just hit the road and see where it took us. Go live somewhere else. Together."

I know where that road leads, but I don't tell him that, either.

"But Janey . . . she . . . she wouldn't stop hitting me. I slapped back and the knife . . ."

A shadow of genuine emotion—the first I've seen him express—flashes his face. I raise my glass and drain it. Then I set it on the bar and slide two twenty-dollar bills beneath it.

"I've got the tab." I rise from the stool.

"Yo!" He grabs my arm, and I allow him to pull me close. "You gonna call the cops? You gonna tell somebody?"

I smile. "No. Your secret is safe with me."

"Bullshit. You're gonna go outside and call someone."

I grab his hand and squeeze. Hard. He flinches. My face is stone as I step away.

"I'll do no such thing," I say. "I have heard your tale and it means nothing to me. Do you think yourself some great murderer? You're not. You're an amateur."

"Fuck you."

"On the contrary. Fuck you. You play at being a killer, but have you murdered anyone since your girlfriend?"

"No."

"Well, there you go. If you really want to transcend, you'll go out tonight and continue your spree."

"You're crazy."

"No. I am the last sane individual in the world."

I leave him sitting there and walk away. I leave the hotel bar and instead of returning to my room, I sit on the smoker's bench outside and keep careful watch on the lobby through the big glass doors. Out on the highway, miles from here, a big rig's air brakes moan. They sound like a ghost.

I only kill out of necessity. I only do what needs to be done. There are doors in our world, and things can come through them. What is an entrance, but an exit? I shut those doors. I close exits.

Eventually, I see him stumble through the lobby, heading for the elevators. He is far too inebriated to notice me re-enter the hotel. He just leans against the wall, waiting for the doors to open. I smile and nod at the desk clerk. The doors slide open. He steps inside, staring at his feet. I join him.

The doors close.

"What floor?" he asks, still looking at his shoes.

I do not answer.

He looks up and I cut his throat before he can scream. It is a practiced stroke. Perfunctory. Clinical. But I grin as I do it, and my heart beats faster than it has in many years.

I am breaking my rules, just this once. I am killing not out of necessity, but out of justice. Out of mercy. This is about putting down a rabid animal.

This is not an exit.

But I am.

Readers have often asked me for a follow-up to "I Am An Exit", so I eventually wrote one. It appeared in my short story collections Unhappy Endings *and* The Little Silver Book of Streetwise Stories. *This tale tells you a little bit more about The Exit (as I've come to call the serial killer)—but not so much as to reveal everything about him. So who is he? Why is he killing people at highway exits? Well, I know, but I ain't telling. Not yet. He was supposed to appear again in my novel* A Gathering of Crows, *but about halfway through the first draft of that novel, I realized that he was stealing the show, so I went back, changed the plot, and wrote him out. You'll see him again in a different, as-yet-unwritten novel. Maybe the rest of his secrets will be revealed there. In fact, I'm sure they will.*

'THE KING',
IN: YELLOW

The man stood rotting on the corner. Frayed rags hung from his skeletal frame and ulcerated sores covered his exposed flesh, weeping blood and pus. He stank. Sweat. Infection. Excrement. Despair.

Finley considered going the long way around him, but Kathryn waved impatiently from across the street. He shouldered by; head down, eyes fixed on the pavement. Invisible.

He can't see me if I can't see him.

"Yo 'zup," the rotting man mumbled over the traffic. "Kin you help a brutha' out wit' a quarta'?"

Finley tried ignoring him, then relented. He didn't have the heart to be so cold, although Kathryn's yuppie friends (they were supposed to be *his* friends too, but he never thought of them that way) would have mocked him for it. He raised his head, actually *looking* at the bum, meeting his watery eyes. They shone. He glanced across the street. Kathryn was incredulous.

"Sorry, man." Finley held his hands out in a pretense of sympathy. "I'm taking my girl to dinner." Feeling like an idiot, he pointed at Kathryn, proving what he was saying was true. "Need to stop at an ATM."

"S'cool," the vagrant smiled. "Ya'll kin hit me on da way back."

"Okay, we'll do that."

He stepped off the curb. The man darted forward, grasping his shoulder. Dirty fingernails clawed at his suit jacket.

"Hey!" Finley protested.

"Have ya'll seen *Yellow*?" the bum croaked.

"No, I don't think so," Finley stammered, clueless.

"Afta' ya' eat, take yo' lady t' see it."

Cackling, he shambled off toward the waterfront.

Kathryn shook her head as Finley crossed the street. "So you met the Human Scab?"

"Only in Baltimore," he grinned.

"Fucking wildlife," she spat, taking his arm. "That's why I take my smoke breaks in the parking garage. I don't know what's worse—the seagulls dive-bombing me, or the homeless dive-bombing me."

81

"The seagulls," Finley replied. "How was your day?"

"Don't try to change the subject, Roger. Christ, you've become so liberal. What happened to the conservative I fell in love with?" She paused and let go of his arm, lighting a cigarette. In the early darkness, the flame lit her face, reminding Finley why he'd fallen in love with her. "But since you asked, it sucked. How was yours?"

"Alright, I guess. Pet Search's site crashed, so I had to un-fuck that. Fed-Ex dropped off my new back-up server. On *Days of Our Lives*, John is still trying to find Stefano and Bo found out about Hope's baby."

"Wish I could work from home. But one of us has to make money."

"Well isn't that why we're going out to dinner? To celebrate your big bonus?"

They crossed Albemarle Street in silence. Ahead, the bright lights of the Inner Harbor beckoned with its fancy restaurants and posh shops. The National Aquarium overlooked the water like an ancient monolith.

Kathryn's brow furrowed.

"Beautiful night," Finley commented, tugging his collar against the cold air blowing in across the water. "You can almost see the stars."

Kathryn said nothing.

"What's wrong?"

She sighed, her breath forming mist in the air. "I feel—I don't know—old. We used to do fun things all the time. Now it's dinner on the couch and whatever's on satellite. Maybe a game of Scrabble if we're feeling energetic."

Finley stared out across the harbor. "I thought you liked coming home every evening with dinner made, and spending a quiet night around the house."

She took his hand.

"I do, Roger. I'm sorry. It's just—we're both thirty now. When was the last time we did something *really* fun?"

"When we were twenty-one and you puked on me during the Depeche Mode concert?"

Kathryn finally laughed, and they walked on, approaching Victor's.

"So why did your day suck?"

"Oh, the lender won't approve the loan on the Spring Grove project because the inspector found black mold in some of the properties. Of course, Ned told him we were going to rip out the tiles during the remodeling phase, but he—"

Finley tuned her out, still nodding and expressing acknowledgement where applicable. After ten years, he'd gotten good at it. When *was* the last time they'd really done something fun? He tried to remember. Didn't this count? Going out to dinner? Probably not. He tried to pinpoint exactly *when* they'd settled into this comfortable zone of domestic familiarity. By mutual agreement, they didn't go to the club anymore. Too many ghetto fabulous suburbanites barely out of college. They didn't go to the movies because she hated the cramped seating and symphony of babies crying and cell phones ringing.

"—so I don't know what I'm going to do," Kathryn finished.

"You'll be fine," Finley nodded, squeezing her hand. "You can handle it."

She smiled, squeezing back.

The line outside Victor's snaked around the restaurant. Finley maneuvered them through it; thankful he'd had the foresight to make reservations. The maitre d' approached them, waving.

"Hello, Ms. Kathryn," he said, clasping her hand. "I'm delighted you could join us."

"Hello, Franklin," she curtsied, smiling as the older man kissed both her cheeks. "This is my boyfriend, Roger."

"A pleasure to make your acquaintance. I've heard much about you."

He winked and Finley grinned, unsure of how to reply.

"Give them a good view," Franklin told the hostess, and turned back to them. "Sheila will seat you. Enjoy your meal."

"I come here a lot for lunch," Kathryn explained as they followed Sheila to their table. "I told Franklin we'd be coming in tonight. He's a nice old guy; a real charmer."

"Yes, he does seem nice," Finley mumbled, distracted. Not for the first time, he found himself surprised by how little he knew about Kathryn's life outside their relationship. He'd never thought to wonder where she spent her lunches.

In many ways, they were different. Strangers making up a whole. She was the consummate twenty-first century yuppie—a corporate lioness intent upon her career and nothing else. He was the epitome of the Generation X slacker, running a home-based web-hosting business. They'd been together almost ten years, but at times, it seemed to him as if they were just coasting. The subjects of marriage and children had been broached several times, and usually deflected by both of them. He needed to devote his time to developing his business. She wasn't where she wanted to be in her career. Despite that, he thought they were happy. So why the disquiet? Maybe Kathryn was right. Maybe they needed to do something fun, something different.

"—at night, isn't it?"

"I'm sorry," he stammered. "What'd you say hon?"

"I said the harbor really is beautiful at night." They were seated in front of a large window, looking out towards the Chesapeake Bay. The lights of the city twinkled in the darkness.

"Yeah, it sure is."

"What were you thinking about, Roger?"

"Honestly? That you're right. We should do something fun. How about we take a trip down to the ocean this weekend? Check out the wild horses, maybe do a little beach-combing?"

"That sounds great," she sighed. "But I can't this weekend. I've got to come in on Saturday and crunch numbers for the Vermont deal. We close on that next week."

"Well then, how about we do something Sunday? Maybe take a drive up to Pennsylvania and visit some of the flea markets, see the Amish, or stop at a produce stand?"

"That's a possibility. Let's play it by ear, okay?"

They studied their menus, basking in the comfortable silence that only long-time partners share. That was when Roger noticed the woman. She and her companion sat at the next table. The flickering candlelight cast shadows on her sallow face. She was thin, almost to the point of emaciation, and there were dark circles under her eyes. Heroin, he wondered, or maybe Anorexia? She obviously came from money. That much was apparent from her jewelry and shoes. Her companion looked wealthy too. Maybe she was a prostitute? No, they seemed too familiar with each other for that.

What caught Finley's attention next was the blood trickling down her leg. Her conversation was animated, and while she gestured excitedly with one hand, the other was beneath the table, clenching her leg. Her fingernails clawed deep into her thigh, hard enough to draw blood. She didn't seem to care. In fact, judging by the look in her eye, she enjoyed the sensation.

Kathryn was absorbed with the menu. He turned back to the couple, and focused on what the woman was saying.

"And then, the King appears. It's such a powerful moment, you can't breathe. I've been to Vegas, and I've seen impersonators, but this guy is the real thing!"

Her companion's response was muffled, and Finley strained to hear.

"I'm serious, Reginald! It's like he's channeling Elvis! The King playing the King! The whole cast is like that. There's a woman who looks and sounds just like Janis Joplin playing the Queen, and a very passable John Lennon as Thale. The best though, next to the King of course, is the guy they cast to play the Pallid Mask. I swear to you Reginald, he's Kurt Cobain! You can't tell the difference. It's all so realistically clever! Actors playing dead rock stars playing roles. A play within a musical within a play."

Her voice dropped to a conspiratorial whisper, and Finley leaned towards them.

"The special effects are amazing. When the Queen has the Pallid Mask tortured, you can actually see little pieces of brain in Cobain's hair. And they have audience participation, too. It's different every night. We each had to reveal a secret that we'd never told anyone. That's why Stephanie left Christopher. Apparently, he revealed a tryst he'd had with a dog when he was thirteen. She left him after the performance. Tonight, I hear they'll be having the audience unmask as well during the masquerade scene!"

He jumped as Kathryn's fingertips brushed his hand.
"Stop eavesdropping," she whispered. "It's not polite."
"Sorry. Have you decided what you're going to have?"
"Mmmm-hmmm," she purred. "I'm going with the crab
cakes. How about you?"
"I think I'll have the filet mignon. Rare. And a big baked
potato with lots of sour cream and butter."
Her eyes widened. "Why Roger, you haven't had that
since your last visit to the doctor. What happened to eating
healthy, so you don't end up like your father?"
"The hell with my hereditary heart disease and
cholesterol!" He closed the menu with a snap. "You said we
need to start having more fun. Red meat and starch is a good
start!"
She laughed, and the lights of the bay reflected in her
eyes. Underneath the table, she slid her foot against his leg.
"I love you, Kathryn."
"I love you too."
The woman at the other table stood up, knocking her
chair backward, and began to scream. Silence, then hushed
murmurs as the woman tottered back and forth on her heels.
Her companion scooted his chair back, cleared his throat in
embarrassment, and reached for her. She slapped his hand
away with a shriek.
"Have you seen the Yellow Sign?" she sang. "Have you
found the Yellow Sign? Have you seen the Yellow Sign?"
She continued the chorus, spinning round and round. Her
flailing arms sent a wine glass crashing to the floor. Her date
lunged for her. She sidestepped, and in one quick movement,
snatched her steak knife from the table and plunged it into
his side. He sank to the floor, pulling the tablecloth and their
meals down with him. The other patrons began screaming as
well. Several dashed for the exit, but no one moved to stop
her. Finley felt frozen in place, transfixed by what occurred
next. Still singing, the woman bent over and plucked up her
soup spoon from the mess on the floor, then used it to gouge
out her eyes. Red and white pulp dribbled down her face.
Voice never wavering, she continued to sing.
Kathryn cringed against Finley. He grabbed her hand,

pulling her toward the exit. Franklin the maitre d', and several men from the kitchen rushed toward the woman. As he hurried Kathryn out the door, he heard the woman cackling.

"I found it! I can see it all! Yhtill, under the stars of Aldebaran and the Hyades! And across the Lake of Hali, on the far shore, lies Carcosa!"

Then they were out the door and into the night. Kathryn sobbed against him, and Finley shuddered. The image of the woman digging into her eye sockets with the soup spoon would not go away.

After they'd given their statement to the police, they walked back to Kathryn's building.

"How could a person do something like that?"

"Drugs maybe," Finley shrugged, "She looked pretty strung out."

"This city gets worse every year."

They arrived back at her office building, and Finley walked around to the side entrance leading into the parking garage. He'd taken the bus, so that they could drive her car back home. Kathryn didn't follow, and he turned to find her stopped under a streetlight.

"What's wrong?"

"I don't think I'm going to be able to sleep tonight."

"Yeah, me either. Let's go home and get you a nice, hot bath. Maybe you'll feel better after that."

"I need a drink."

"We can stop off at the liquor store—"

"No," she cut him off. "I need to be around people, Roger. I need to hear music and laughter and forget about that insane bitch."

"You want to hit a club?" He heard the surprised tone in his voice.

"I don't know what I want, but I know that I don't want to go home right now. Let's walk over to Fell's Point and see what we can find."

Part of Baltimore's harbor district, the buildings in Fell's Point had been old when Edgar Allan Poe was new to the city. By day, it was a tourist trap; six blocks of antique shops

87

and bookstores and curio dealers. Urban chic spawned and bred in its coffee shops and cafes. At night, the college crowd descended upon it, flocking to any of the dozens of nightclubs and bars that dotted the area.

They strolled down Pratt Street, arms linked around each other's waist, and Finley smiled.

A figure lurched out of the shadows. "Have ya'll seen Yellow?"

Finley groaned. He'd forgotten about the homeless man—the Human Scab. He thrust his hand into his pants pocket and pulled out a rumpled five.

"Here," he said, offering it to the rotting man. "I promised you I'd get you on the way back. Now if you don't mind, my girlfriend and I have had a rough evening."

"Thanks yo. Sorry t' hear 'bout yo night. I'm tellin' ya', take yer girl ta' see Yellow. Dat'll fix ya right up." With one dirty, ragged finger, he pointed at a poster hanging from a light pole. "Ya'll have a good 'un."

The bum shuffled off into the darkness, humming a snatch of melody. Finley recognized the tune as "Are You Lonesome Tonight." He shuddered, reminded of the crazy woman at the restaurant, raving about the Elvis impersonator that she'd seen. He tried to remember what it was she had been singing, but all that came to mind was the image of her gored face.

The eight by ten poster had been made to look like it was printed on a snake's skin. Over the scales, pale lettering read:

Hastur Productions Proudly Presents:

YELLOW
(The Awful Tragedy of Young Castaigne)

Banned in Paris, Munich, London, and Rome, we are proud to bring this classic 19th century play to Baltimore, in its only U.S. appearance! Filled with music, emotion and dark wonder, YELLOW is an unforgettable and mystifying tale!

Not to be missed!

Starring:

Sid Vicious as Uoht
John Lennon as Thale
Mama Cass as Cassilda
Janis Joplin as The Queen
Karen Carpenter as Camilla
James Marshall Hendrix as Alar
Jim Morrison as Aldones, the Lizard King
Kurt Cobain as The Pallid Mask, or,
Phantom of Truth
and
Elvis Presley as The King

Also featuring: Robert Johnson, Bon
Scott, Roy Orbison, Freddy Mercury,
Cliff Burton, Dimebag Darrell, Johnny
Cash and more.

One Week Only! Nightly Performances
Begin Promptly at Midnight

The R.W. Chambers Theatre
Fells Point, corner of Fedogan St. &
Bremer Ave.
Baltimore, MD

The breeze coming off the harbor chilled him. This was what the crazy woman had been talking about—actors depicting dead musicians depicting characters in a play. *This* play. The same play the bum had recommended. The coincidence was unsettling.

"Sounds like fun, doesn't it?" Kathryn asked. "You should have tipped him more money."

"Only in Baltimore can the homeless get jobs as ushers. Come on, let's find a pub."

"No, let's go see this! Look, they've got actors pretending to be dead musicians playing actors. How cool is that?" She giggled, and looked at him pleadingly.

He told her what he'd overheard the woman say.

"Then that's all the more reason," she insisted. "Once people read about the connection in tomorrow's Baltimore Sun, we won't be able to get tickets because of the demand. People love morbid stuff like that!"

"Don't you think it's odd that this all happened in the same night? You said you wanted to forget about what happened. Don't you think that attending a play that this same woman went to will just make it that more vivid?"

"Roger, you said that you agreed with me; that we never do anything fun anymore, that we're not spontaneous. Here's our chance! How much more spur-of-the-moment can we get?"

"Kathryn, it's almost eleven-thirty! It's late."

"The poster says it doesn't start until midnight."

Finley sighed in reluctance. "Alright, we'll go to the play. You're right, it might be fun."

He allowed her to lead him down the street and into Fells Point.

The R. W. Chambers Theatre wasn't just off the beaten path—it was far, far beyond it. They picked their way through a maze of winding, twisting streets and alleyways, each more narrow than the previous. The throng of drunken college kids and office interns vanished, replaced by the occasional rat or pigeon. Kathryn's heels clicked on the cobblestones, each step sounding like a rifle shot.

This is the old part of the city, Finley thought. *The oldest. The dark heart.*

The very atmosphere seemed to echo his discomfort, accentuating it as they went farther. There were no streetlights in this section, and no lights shining in the windows of the houses. The buildings crowded together; crumbling statues of crumbling nineteenth century architecture. The street smelled faintly of garbage and stale urine, and the only sound was that of dripping water, and of something small scuttling in the darkness. Kathryn gripped his hand tightly, and then—

—they emerged onto the corner, and the lights and noise flooded back again. A crowd milled about in front of the theatre.

Finley's apprehension dissipated, and he chided himself for being silly. At the same time, Kathryn's grip loosened.

"Look at this crowd!" Kathryn exclaimed. "It's more popular than we thought."

"Word of mouth must have spread fast."

"Maybe your homeless friend has been pimping it."

Finley grinned. "Maybe."

They took their place at the end of the line, behind a young Goth couple. The theatre had seen better days. The water-stained brickwork looked tired and faded. Several windows on the second floor had been boarded over, and the others were dark. Some of the light bulbs in the marquee had burned out, but *HASTUR PRODUCTIONS' YELLOW* and the show time and ticket prices were prominently visible. One side of the building was plastered with paper billboards promoting the play. Others advertised bands with names like Your Kid's On Fire, Suicide Run, and I, Chaos.

The line snaked forward, and finally it was their turn. Finley stared at the man behind the glass window of the ticket booth. His skin was pale, almost opaque, and tiny blue veins spider-webbed his face and hands. Gray lips flopped like two pieces of raw liver as he spoke.

"Enjoy the performance."

Finley nodded. Placing his arm around Kathryn's waist, he guided them into the building. The usher in the lobby had the same alabaster complexion, and was slightly more laconic than his sullen ticket booth counterpart. Without a word, he took their tickets, handed back the stubs and two programs, then silently parted a pair of black curtains and gestured for them to enter.

The theatre filled quickly. They found a spot midway down the center aisle. The red velvet-covered chairs squeaked as they sat down.

"I can't get over it," Kathryn whispered. "Look at all these people!"

Finley studied the program booklet. Like the posters, it was designed to appear as if it had been bound in serpent skin. He struggled to read the pale lettering.

"YELLOW was written in the late 19th century by a young playwright named Castaigne. Tragically, Castaigne took his own life immediately upon completing the work. When YELLOW was first published and performed, the city of Paris banned the play, followed by Munich and London, and eventually most of the world's governments and churches. It was translated in 1930 by the scholar Daniel Mason Winfield-Harms; who, in a strange twist of fate echoing that of the original author, was found dead in Buffalo, New York after finishing the adaptation. YELLOW takes place, not on Earth, but on another world, in the city of Yhtill, on the shore of the Lake of Hali, under the stars of Aldebaran and Hyades."

Kathryn stirred next to him. "You know what this reminds me of?"

"What?"

"When I was in high school. At midnight on Saturdays, we'd go to see *The Rocky Horror Picture Show*. It has that feel to it."

"Maybe they'll sing 'The Time Warp.'"

She reached over and squeezed his hand, and Finley felt good. Happy.

The lights dimmed, plunging them into darkness. The crowd grew silent as a burst of static coughed from the overhead speakers. Then, an eerie, unfamiliar style of music began. A light appeared at the back of the theatre. The performers entered from the rear, each of them carrying a single candle. The troupe walked slowly down the center aisle, singing as they approached the stage.

"Have you seen the Yellow Sign? Have you found the Yellow Sign?"

As they passed by, Finley forcibly resisting the urge to reach out and touch them. The resemblance to their dead alter egos was uncanny. The actress playing Janis Joplin (playing the Queen) was a *perfect* duplicate, down to the blue-tinged skin that must have adorned her face in death. Following her were Jim Morrison (a bloated Aldones) and John Lennon (a Thale with fresh bloodstains on his clothing). Mama Cass, Jimi Hendrix, Sid Vicious—the procession continued, until two-dozen actors had taken the stage.

"Look at that!" Kathryn pointed to the quarter-sized drops of blood left in the Lennon actor's wake. "Gruesome. I can't wait to see what they did with Kurt Cobain . . ."

Finley shuddered. "Good special effects, that's for sure."

The singing swelled, the upraised voices echoing like thunder. "Have you seen the Yellow Sign? Have you found the Yellow Sign? Let the red dawn surmise what we shall do, when this blue starlight dies and all is through. Have you seen the Yellow Sign? Have you found the Yellow Sign?"

They repeated the chorus two more times. On the last note, the candles were extinguished and the lights on the stage grew brighter.

The first part of the play concerned the intrigue of the royal court. The aging Queen was pestered and plied by her children: Cassilda, Alar, Camilla, Thale, Uoht, and Aldones, all claimants for the throne to Yhtill. They vied for the crown, so that the dynasty would continue, each one claiming to be to be the rightful successor. Despite their efforts, the Queen declined to give the crown away. Mama Cass began to sing, and Finley's skin prickled.

"Along the shore the cloud waves break. The twin suns sink behind the lake. The shadows lengthen, in Carcosa. Strange is the night where black stars rise, and strange moons circle through the skies. But stranger still is lost Carcosa. Songs that the Hyades shall sing, where flap the tatters of the King, must die unheard in dim Carcosa. Song of my soul, my voice is dead, die though, unsung, as tears unshed shall dry and die in lost Carcosa."

The crowd applauded, enraptured with her performance. Then the Cobain character appeared on stage, his face hidden beneath a pallid mask. When he turned his back to the audience, the crowd gasped. Hair and skull were gone, offering a glimpse of gray matter.

Finley had trouble following the plot after that.

Cobain's character, the Phantom of Truth, pronounced doom upon the Queen and her subjects. The threat apparently came from a non-existent city that would appear on the other side of the lake. Reacting to this news, the Queen ordered him tortured.

Though Kathryn seemed enraptured, Finley grew restless as it continued. He found it incoherent to the point of absurdity. One moment, a character professed their love for another. The next, they discussed a race of people who lacked anuses, and could consume only milk, evacuating their waste through vomiting. The characters rambled on, and Finley slipped into a half conscious state—his mind adrift with other matters but the actor's lines droned on in the back of his head.

"There are so many things which are impossible to explain! Why should certain chords of music make me think of the brown and golden tints of autumn foliage?"

"Let the red dawn surmise . . ."

"Aldebaran and the Hyades have aligned, my Queen!"

"What we shall do . . ."

"Sleep now, the blessed sleep, and be not troubled by these ill omens."

"When this blue starlight dies . . ."

"The City of Carcosa has appeared on the other side of Lake Hali!"

"And all is through . . ."

He wasn't sure how long he stayed like that; head drooping and eyes half shut. Kathryn's light laughter and the chuckles coming from the rest of the audience startled him awake again. He checked his watch; then glanced around at the other patrons. Immediately, his attention focused on a couple behind them. The woman's head was in her lover's lap, bobbing up and down in the darkness. Before he could tell Kathryn, he noticed another display; this one in their own row. A man at the end was lovingly biting another man's ear, hard enough to draw blood. His partner licked his lips in ecstasy.

"Kathryn—" he whispered.

She shushed him and focused on the play, her face rapt with attention. Her cheeks were flushed, and Finley noticed that her nipples stood out hard against her blouse. Without a word, her hand fell into his lap and began to stroke him through his pants. Despite the bizarre mood permeating the theatre, he felt himself harden.

Just then, there was a commotion at the back of the

theatre, as another actor entered. The crowd turned as the actors pointed with mock cries of shock and dismay. He wore a gilded robe with scarlet fringes, and a clasp of black onyx, on which was inlaid a curious symbol of gold. Though his face was hidden beneath a pallid mask identical to the one Cobain was wearing, there was no mistaking the trademark swagger. He swept down the aisle, pausing as the crowd burst into spontaneous applause.

"Thank you. Thank you very much."

He bowed to the audience, and then took the stage in three quick strides.

"Behold, the Yellow Sign upon his breast!" cried the Queen. "It is the King of Carcosa, and he seeks the Phantom of Truth!"

Hendrix, Lennon, and Vicious entered the audience, each with a burlap bag slung over their shoulders.

"Masks!" they called. "Everyone receive your masks! No pushing. There's plenty for everyone!"

Finley pushed Kathryn's hand away in alarm. They were passing out *knives*—real knives rather than stage props. The lights glinted off the serrated blades.

"Kathryn, we—"

His statement was cut short as her mouth covered his. Greedily, she sucked at his tongue, her body suddenly filling his lap. The scene replayed itself throughout the theatre. Men and women, men and men, women and women. Couples, threesomes, and more. Clothes were discarded, and naked, glistening bodies entwined around each other in the seats and on the floor. All the while, the dead rock stars waded through the crowd, dispensing knives.

"Kathryn, stop it!" He pushed her away. "Something is really fucked up here."

"Have you found it, Roger? Have you seen the Yellow Sign?"

"What?"

She slapped him. Hard. Then, grinning, she slapped him again.

"Now, you slap me," she urged. "Come on, Roger. You said you wanted to do something different. Make me wet. Hit me!"

95

"No!"

"Coward! Pussy! You limp dick mother-fucker! Do it, or I'll find someone else here who will!"

"What the hell is wrong with you?"

It's like she's hypnotized or something! All of them are! What the hell happened while I was asleep?

On stage, what appeared to be a masked ball scene was underway.

"You have questioned him to no avail!" Elvis' voice rang out through the hall, echoing over the mingled cries of pain and ecstasy. He was addressing the actors, but at the same time, the audience as well. "Time to unmask. All must show their true faces! All! Except for myself. For indeed, I wear no mask at all!"

As one, the crowd picked up their knives and began to flay the skin from their faces. Some laughed as they did it. Others helped the person sitting next to them. Finley turned, just as Kathryn slid the blade through one cheek. A loose flap of skin hung down past her chin.

"Kathryn, don't!"

He grabbed for the knife and she jerked it away. Before he could move, she slashed at his hands. Blood welled in his palm as he dodged another slice. Then he slapped her, leaving a bloody handprint on her cheek.

"That's it baby!" she shrieked. "Let me finish taking my mask off, and then I'll help you with yours."

"All unmask!" Elvis boomed again, and Finley turned to the stage, unable to look away. The King removed the Pallid Mask concealing his face, and what he revealed wasn't Elvis. It wasn't even human. Beneath the mask was a head like that of a puffy grave worm. It lolled obscenely, surveying the crowd, then gave a strange, warbling cry.

Kathryn's skin landed on the floor with a wet sound.

The thing on stage turned toward Finley, and then he saw. He saw it. He found it.

Roger Finley screamed.

"Excuse me?" The bum shuffled forward.

"Just ignore him, Marianne. If we give him money, he'll

hound us the whole way to the harbor."

"Don't be ridiculous, Thomas," the woman scolded her husband. "The poor fellow looks half starved. And he's articulate for a street person!"

The bum shuffled eagerly from foot to foot while she reached within her purse and pulled out a five-dollar bill. She placed it in his outstretched hand.

"Here you go. Please see to it that you get a hot meal, now. No alcohol or drugs."

"Thank you. Much obliged. Since you folks were so kind, let me help you out."

"We don't need any help, thank you very much." The husband stiffened, wary of the homeless man's advances.

"Just wanted to give you a tip. If you like the theatre, you should take your wife to see *Yellow*."

He pointed at a nearby poster. The couple thanked him and walked away, but not before stopping to read the poster for themselves.

Roger Finley pocketed the five dollars, and watched them disappear into Fell's Point, in search of the Yellow Sign. He wondered if they would find it, and if so, what they would see.

This is, of course, a tribute to Robert W. Chambers' classic of the same name. But you already knew that because you've read the Chambers' story, right? Nope. I've got twenty bucks that says half of you have never even heard of Robert W. Chambers. And that, my friends, is just wrong.

True story. Thirteen years ago, at the first Horrorfind Weekend Convention, J. F. Gonzalez and I were approached by a young man; probably in his early twenties. He shook our hands and said nice things about our books, and called us inspirations. How the hell we, two of the lynchpins of the so-called gangsta horror movement, were inspirations is beyond me, but hey, the kid was sincere enough to buy Jesus (which is J.F.'s real name) a beer and me a shot of tequila. We started talking about writing, and we were trying to give him some advice. The conversation turned to the masters of the genre, and we were horrified to learn that this kid had never read Chambers, never read Hodgson, never read James, never read Machen, and had only a dim knowledge of Lovecraft. The final straw was when we moved to the more modern era, and the kid admitted that he'd never heard of Karl Edward Wagner.

Once I'd removed J. F.'s hands from around his throat ("How can you not know who Karl Edward Fucking Wagner is?" he screamed while throttling him), we sent the young writer on his way and proceeded to grumble about "These damn kids!" for the rest of the day.

If you don't know those names I mentioned above, you need to correct that. Now. Horror fiction has a rich history, and it is your heritage as a fan, as a reader, and especially if you're a writer. Seek it out. Learn from it. M. R. James. William Hope Hodgson (one of my favorites). Lord Dunsany. Arthur Machen. Clark Ashton Smith. Edward Lucas White. Ambrose Bierce (another one of my favorites). Hell, explore the modern era, with John Farris and Robert Bloch and so many others. And for God's sake—learn who Karl Edward Wagner was so that J. F. Gonzalez doesn't throttle you next. Seriously, go look for this stuff. Read it. You'll be glad you did.

As for the story itself, I got the idea while walking around Fell's Point in Baltimore. At the time, I was still shocked that the kid had never read Robert W. Chambers. Things came together and the story came out in one sitting. It was originally published in one of John Pelan's Darkside anthologies and was reprinted in my out-of-print short story collection Fear of Gravity.

BRIAN KEENE is the author of over twenty-five books, including *Darkness on the Edge of Town, Urban Gothic, Castaways, Kill Whitey, Dark Hollow, Dead Sea, Ghoul* and *The Rising*. He also writes comic books such as *The Last Zombie, Doom Patrol* and *Dead of Night: Devil Slayer*. His work has been translated into German, Spanish, Polish, Italian, French and Taiwanese. Several of his novels and stories have been optioned for film, one of which, *The Ties That Bind*, premiered on DVD in 2009 as a critically-acclaimed independent short. Keene's work has been praised in such diverse places as *The New York Times*, The History Channel, The Howard Stern Show, CNN.com, *Publisher's Weekly, Fangoria Magazine*, and *Rue Morgue Magazine*. Keene lives in Central Pennsylvania. You can communicate with him online at www.briankeene.com, on Facebook at www.facebook.com/pages/Brian-Keene/189077221397 or on Twitter at www.twitter.com/BrianKeene

deadite press

"Brain Cheese Buffet" Edward Lee - collecting nine of Lee's most sought after tales of violence and body fluids. Featuring the Stoker nominated "Mr. Torso," the legendary gross-out piece "The Dritiphilist," the notorious "The McCrath Model SS40-C, Series S," and six more stories to test your gag reflex.

"Edward Lee's writing is fast and mean as a chain saw revved to full-tilt boogie."

- Jack Ketchum

"Bullet Through Your Face" Edward Lee - No writer is more extreme, perverted, or gross than Edward Lee. His world is one of psychopathic redneck rapists, sex addicted demons, and semen stealing aliens. Brace yourself, the king of splatterspunk is guaranteed to shock, offend, and make you laugh until you vomit.

"Lee pulls no punches."

- Fangoria

"Whargoul" Dave Brockie - It is a beast born in bullets and shrapnel, feeding off of pain, misery, and hard drugs. Cursed to wander the Earth without the hope of death, it is reborn again and again to spread the gospel of hate, abuse, and genocide. But what if it's not the only monster out there? What if there's something worse? From Dave Brockie, the twisted genius behind GWAR, comes a novel about the darkest days of the twentieth century.

"Clickers" J. F. Gonzalez and Mark Williams- They are the Clickers, giant venomous blood-thirsty crabs from the depths of the sea. The only warning to their rampage of dismemberment and death is the terrible clicking of their claws. But these monsters aren't merely here to ravage and pillage. They are being driven onto land by fear. Something is hunting the Clickers. Something ancient and without mercy. *Clickers* is J. F. Gonzalez and Mark Williams' gore-soaked cult classic tribute to the giant monster B-movies of yesteryear.

"Clickers II" J. F. Gonzalez and Brian Keene- Thousands of Clickers swarm across the entire nation and march inland, slaughtering anyone and anything they come across. But this time the Clickers aren't blindly rushing onto land - they are being led by an intelligence older than civilization itself. A force that wants to take dry land away from the mammals. Those left alive soon realize that they must do everything and anything they can to protect humanity – no matter the cost. This isn't war, this is extermination.

"Urban Gothic" Brian Keene - When their car broke down in a dangerous inner-city neighborhood, Kerri and her friends thought they would find shelter inside an old, dark row home. They thought they would be safe there until help arrived. They were wrong. The residents who live down in the cellar and the tunnels beneath the city are far more dangerous than the streets outside, and they have a very special way of dealing with trespassers. Trapped in a world of darkness, populated by obscene abominations, they will have to fight back if they ever want to see the sun again.

"Trolley No. 1852" Edward Lee - In 1934, horror writer H.P. Lovecraft is invited to write a story for a subversive underground magazine, all on the condition that a pseudonym will be used. The pay is lofty, and God knows, Lovecraft needs the money. There's just one catch. It has to be a pornographic story . . . The 1852 Club is a bordello unlike any other. Its women are the most beautiful and they will do anything. But there is something else going on at this sex club. In the back rooms monsters are performing vile acts on each other and doors to other dimensions are opening . . .

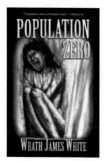

"Population Zero" Wrath James White - An intense sadistic tale of how one man will save the world through sterilization. *Population Zero* is the story of an environmental activist named Todd Hammerstein who is on a mission to save the planet. In just 50 years the population of the planet is expected to double. But not if Todd can help it. From Wrath James White, the celebrated master of sex and splatter, comes a tale of environmentalism, drugs, and genital mutilation.

AVAILABLE FROM AMAZON.COM

Lightning Source UK Ltd.
Milton Keynes UK

173283UK00008BA/53/P